# APOLLO'S
# CHILD

JOAN SMITH

# APOLLO'S CHILD

## Julia MacRae Books

A DIVISION OF WALKER BOOKS

ACKNOWLEDGEMENTS
In researching for this novel, I would like to
acknowledge a debt to: *Hippocratic Writings*,
edited by G.E.R. Lloyd (Pelican); *Hippocrates* by
W.H.S. Jones (Loeb edition); *Everyday Things in
Ancient Greece* by Marjorie & C.H.B. Quennell,
(Batsford) and *Greece* 478–336 Open University
Course A292.

First published in Great Britain 1989
by Julia MacRae Books
A division of Walker Books Ltd
87 Vauxhall Walk, London, SE11 5HJ

British Library Cataloguing in Publication Data

Smith, Joan, *1933*–
Apollo's child.
I. Title
823'.914 [J]
ISBN 0-86203-411-6


Printed and bound in Great Britain by
Billings and Sons Ltd., Worcester

*The Island of Cos, 418 BC*

# CHAPTER ONE

I am ahead of Timocrates.

Any moment he will catch me. Past the third cypress from the big rock. The second. Fifteen strides to the first. My chest will burst. Five strides. Still Timocrates does not move forward. The last cypress tree. The winning post is mine.

Flat on my back, heaving, I crow, "I...beat... you...Timocrates. I...did...it." Fists drum the dew-cold grass, "I did it." The wet dandelions brush my skin, flints spite my shoulders. No matter. I have beaten Timocrates. My heart is huge with joy.

Timocrates says nothing, his head buried in the thyme. At last he looks up.

"This one time, Philo. Never again." He stares at me with aggressive pride. "Besides, I need tough opposition if I am to take the crown at Olympia."

We sit up, I still smug. Far below us, Astipalea comes alive. Already traders, small as tapestry needles, quarrel at the quay as they haul ashore the nets restless with fish. Oil, wine and silk stand in piles for when the caiques, the small trading boats, arrive. Men scuttle, like demented white ants, round the market tables. And beyond the edge of the land, a rock hurled into the sea by Poseidon in one of his moods, the island of Nissiros slowly reveals its June-grape bloom of lavender and watery green through the mist.

This is my favourite time. Timocrates and I come to

train over the rough hillside, to prepare for that great day which lies ahead, the one we dream about all the time. My dream is perfect, but Timocrates is too practical.

"It is no good, Philo." He sucks a piece of grass, making it squeak as he pulls it through his teeth. "We must face up to it." He worries me when he is in this mood. He grabs a slim fallen branch, and picks off the bark until it is smooth. He always fidgets.

"When we leave school?"

"Dreams do not happen. They evaporate."

"You have to be rich. We will never be that."

"Philo, we *will* run at Olympia. We *will* walk through the great arch that leads into the stadium. That arch at Olympia divides the excellent from the common. The crowds launch your name onto the air and the sound will stay forever in your ear."

"We will win all the crowns of wild olive." I raise my arms to acknowledge the applause.

"You are a pathetic dreamer." Timocrates coils himself like a spring, then hoists the stick into the sky as if it were a javelin.

The stick shudders into the air and falls a few lengths ahead. Rough branches cannot be javelins. And poor boys do not compete at Olympia.

Timocrates kicks the useless branch, stubs his toe, and regrets it. "The rich do not have to work. They train each afternoon, and grow strong. They are noted in the stadium. But I am to work hidden in the foundry. I will never be seen."

We are the poorest boys I know. Timocrates laces his feet to look as if he wears shoes, but there are no soles bound on. It is the wonder of the town that either of us gets sent to school, Timocrates with no father at all,

8

and me, the son of a man who sells thongs in the market. But the town knows nothing. If the rich are proud, the poor must be prouder still.

"It is for the gods, Timocrates. Maybe..."

The world below is garlanded with swags of pearl haze, like the view from Mount Olympus itself, and I have beaten Timocrates in a sprint. The smile of the gods, perhaps of Apollo himself, graces me.

"The gods! Apollo? Great Zeus? Poseidon? *They* do not know I am here." Timocrates starts off down the hill, skidding deliberately on the wet tussocks.

He stops, balances on a boulder like an ibex, as certain and controlled as the wild goat. "I am going to Olympia," he says. "And I do not need the gods to take me there."

Timocrates is tall and lean and when he runs his skin has a glow like a healthy horse. He looks like a god himself, with the light from the east behind him, shining luminous about his figure dark against the morning. He looks like Apollo, symbol of beauty and reason, god of medicine. No. He does not. Timocrates looks savage.

By comparison, I am small and my hair is like a patch of corn, rain rumpled, not combed by the sun. As well as training for Olympia, I run to make me taller, more distinguished.

We get down to the town and reach the market place where the names of the heroes are written up, and see statues of men with horses. Horses are only for the rich. The marble faces wear the disdain of the aristocrats.

"When I win the crown of wild olive at Olympia," says Timocrates, "the town will put up a statue of me here. Parien marble and gilded."

The marble athletes sneer. Here, where money jangles, we are nothing. And I wish I were up in the hills still, among the clean mists where dreams are all quite possible.

My father is already at his stall. I see him immediately, a head taller than any man there. Around him, traders are at their busiest. The live chickens grow noisy; the dead chickens begin to smell. The frantic hustle round the tables contrasts with the restrained conversations in the colonnade.

His tunic may be only wool, but here stands the finest man in the market, with his wide shoulders sculptured in youth by fighting the Spartans. His heavy, curly head is like a bull's. He spots a friend; his eyes sparkle.

"Got your dice with you?" bellows Father across two stalls, in a voice so powerful it could knock Zeus off Olympus. He turns back to a customer in a dazzling cotton tunic who is examining thongs with a hand so white it might be that of a lady. He is a councillor, but would be nothing if *my* father were to speak in the assembly.

Last night, my father cut thongs from scrounged leather remnants far into the night, so that I, his son, might go to school. The thongs are laid out now according to their strengths and lengths, beside the side-lines of eggs and scones and cabbages.

"Not my quality," sniffs the councillor and minces away.

Father laughs, a huge roar like thunder echoing in the mountains. The laugh ends in a cough which makes him laugh some more. He sees us and beckons.

He makes a huge fist and pretends to box my ears,

gentle as the kiss of a butterfly. "Made my mind up."

"What about?"

"Your future, my son. Your further education."

"We have no money for more education, Father."

He puts his arm across my shoulders. It is a mighty weight.

"You can be successful. A force in the world. A credit to me. Speak in the assembly. Would I throw that away now?"

"There is no more furniture to sell. You must never sell the couch."

"No more I shall. That is your inheritance. But I have thought hard. I shall strike a bargain with the tall thin one." Father points to the colonnade.

A white-robed sophist, a travelling teacher, threads his path through the stalls on his way to the marble shade, to where the businessmen contract and philosophers argue with their students to teach the skills of debate.

"My daily supply of eggs for a fee," says Father. "To make you what I should have been. A man who can address the assembly. Be admired. Be envied."

"Would eggs be suitable?"

"Everyone needs eggs, Philo. A sensible arrangement, I would say."

"We cannot afford to give eggs away."

"Teach you manners. The art of conversation. Give you nobility of mind, my son, and great wisdom." His eyes sparkle with the joy of giving.

"And tricks of speech," says Timocrates.

"Off to school with you, and I will speak to him straight away."

We leave Father puffing himself up to approach the sophist, brushing down his tunic ready to use all his powers of persuasion, all the charm of his voice and ready smile. And his sense of what should be. My father is a fine man.

Timocrates is not my friend now. His face is bitter. He strides ahead, head tilted back and his eyelids low, veiling his jealousy.

"So you are to be as a rich man's son," he sneers.

"No, Timocrates. My father will never get me an education without money."

"Talking in the morning, learning how to twist words to influence other people. In the gymnasium every afternoon with all the other men of letters. Running. Wrestling. Growing stronger. And I get no chance at all."

"But my father..."

Suddenly Timocrates speaks of a matter quite new. "My father... *my* father was a rich and important man. He truly loved my mother, but he could not marry her. He was an Athenian citizen, and must marry a woman also of the city of Athens."

"You have never said you were a rich man's son." I do not know whether to believe this.

"Am I likely to refer often to my mother's unmarried state?"

"Sorry. No."

"And I know he loved her. Because of the necklace. She keeps it locked away and hidden. Sometimes she gets it out and looks at it. Gold, with emeralds. Pure gold, and the stones glow like the sea at dawn. However poor we get, I know she will never sell it."

"Does *he* know about you?"

"Who do you think pays for school?"

"Then he could pay a sophist."

He ignores me, and I know his father has now

lost interest.

"It makes me proud," says Timocrates, "that I bear his name."

We reach the edge of the market, and Timocrates strides on. He is once more certain that he will grasp that briefest one-day glory, in the glow of which a man might stay warm for the rest of his life. He has that arrogance about him, even at this moment, for which a father will pay half a fortune to have instilled into his son, an arrogance without effort, even despite bare feet.

After school, I return to our house, which is larger than might be expected of a thong seller. There were many years of good corn harvests after the Persian wars. During that time, my grandfather, like many men with a piece of land, grew rich. Sadly, the good times never last.

Now the land is sold, the money gone, and only the house belongs to the family. There was fine furniture once, the carved chest and some elegant chairs with curved legs, but that has been sold to send me to school. There still remains the couch on which Father sleeps. The legs are carved with Ionic scrolls, and there is a meander border to the head, and pineapples for decoration. It is the couch that reminds my father he is not a common man; once there was excellence.

We are poor but, according to Agatha my aunt, two threads tie us to what matters in this world which is a proper standing in the eyes of others. We are insecurely linked to respectability by the size of our house and also by Xenia. Yes, we do have a slave, though Xenia rarely behaves like one.

She runs to me now across the yard, her wayward

hair only partly restrained by a band of plaited red wool, and grabs me by the arm. "You did not wait for me this morning. I wanted to come with you, and run in the hills."

"I told you, Xenia, it would not be seemly. You are almost a woman. Besides, you could never keep up with Timocrates and me."

"I could. Easily. I stayed awake half the night to hear you leave. But I had a little nod, and you were gone."

"You had the fire to kindle. Bread to bake."

"Ah, the bread. The bread is not my fault. I was thinking of running in the hills." Through the store-room window I see the black-topped loaves. Xenia's domestic disasters are a feature of our house.

"I will come with you tomorrow."

"You will not."

She stands in front of me, bubbling with fury, like a pot of oil on the fire. She returns to the store-room with her bouncing, certain tread. I see a hand appear and take a loaf from the sill where it is cooling, and hear muffled scrunching as Xenia tries to de-scab the black loaves.

Yes, we have a slave, but not because we can *afford* a servant. Xenia is not a sign of our affluence.

She is the granddaughter of one of Grandfather's slaves from Anatolia, one among many of the spoils of the Persian war. Xenia, orphaned at birth, was brought up by my mother, for there was no one else to care for her. It is not always easy to remember that Xenia is a slave.

Take the afternoon when I was about six and Xenia no more than four. She was always trouble, especially then, tangling the spun wool, exploring the jars in the store-room, tormenting the hens.

Agatha lost her temper, and spanked her hard. "Another child, in your circumstances, would have been exposed on the hillside and left to die. We would have none of this trouble today if that had been done." Agatha plonked a screaming Xenia down on the ground.

"What did you say?" I cannot have heard it right.

Mother, coming out to see what the noise was about, tried to explain. "You see, Philo, a baby is no use as a slave, indeed it is another mouth to feed. Such a baby will often be put out on the hillside..." She could not finish.

"And left to die?"

"There is no law against it. The baby might live. Never mind, I could not do that to the small creature. She was such a pretty little thing right from the day she was born."

"She would have died if it were not for you, Mother."

Agatha was looking very self-righteous, folding up a blanket.

"Definitely," she said. "And we regret it now, and none more than those poor hens."

I remember taking the small child from Mother and holding her to myself. Eventually, Xenia stopped bellowing and looked up at me. For many days afterwards I watched that she came to no harm. It must have been then that I found the knuckle bones, and began to teach her the skill of the game.

Now Xenia emerges from the store-room, looking pleased, and only slightly crumb-specked. "I forgot. Could you go and fetch your aunt?"

"Fetch her from where?"

"She is sitting in the road, just this side of the fountain house."

"Agatha sitting in the road?"

"A cat ran in front of her. It was an omen, you see. She says she cannot possibly move until someone else passes. All the women who were at the fountain house realise what has happened, and walk another way home, to annoy her."

"Why could you not walk past her?"

"I did, but she says slaves do not count."

I go to retrieve Agatha, my father's sister, who, not surprisingly, has never been claimed in marriage. "A black day," she reports. "Black as a crow."

"I am sure a *good* omen will crop up soon, Agatha, though no doubt you will ignore that."

I haul her to her feet, and lead her back to the house.

"Of course, if your father earned a proper wage I would not have to go myself to the fountain house," she says.

"Father works very hard. It is not his fault thongs make so little money."

"Thongs do not buy respect," sniffs Agatha. "And I doubt you will do any better."

I know my father is not an ordinary man. I know him by his heart which is great, and not by the thongs which create no envy.

Xenia has forgotten her annoyance at not running in the hills by the time Agatha and I return, but has other things on her mind. "Have you brought your slate home?"

"It was a mess, I smoothed out the wax."

"Philo. You know I want to learn what you have learned. Being a woman should not keep me ignorant. I am much cleverer than you are. I need to learn everything. For when I become free."

"Men will always be better than women, Xenia. That is how it is."

"I am better with these for a start." She picks up the five knuckle bones I gave her when she was four summers old, and throws them up, as I taught her myself. Xenia catches them all now, and hands them to me.

I throw them up. Some skid around the yard.

"Three. There you are, you see. You taught me and now I am better than my teacher."

"You have practised. Besides, it is a child's game."

Xenia's face crinkles with joy. "To a man, a child's game should be as nothing."

I pick her up, and dump her in the store-room among the new bread. By the time I have struggled with the key to lock the door, she has climbed out of the window.

Agatha comes out of the weaving room and clasps her head in despair. "You are a harpy," she screeches. "Good for no-one. And look at that bread. No crust at all, now."

"You should bake the bread, then," says Xenia.

"Not the task," says Agatha, "for one who could have been a lady."

Xenia and I sit under the vine in the yard, and she tries to teach me how to play knuckle bones, as I once taught her.

"Could you imagine me addressing the assembly?"

"No."

"Why not?"

"You are too honest."

"You know nothing about politics."

Xenia looks at me as if she thinks she does, which is annoying. Because she says nothing, I burble on about Father speaking to a sophist about my further education. "There is no limit to what I might do. Commerce. Politics. Become a philosopher."

Xenia should be full of admiration. She should look up to her superior. I wonder if she will laugh instead but her face is serious now.

"Well?"

"That is only the person the world sees."

"So?"

"The spirit is more important, and knows nothing of assemblies."

"You say that only because women do not sit in the assembly. Slaves neither."

My mother comes into the yard and glances towards the gate. "I hear your father's step," she says, and touches her hair, checking that it is smooth.

She will always be beautiful because of her thick hair, unusually fair, however many darns pattern her robe or how ever rough her hands may be with work nature did not design for her.

Father stands at the gate. He looks tired, not the same man who bellowed to his friends across the stalls. He comes over, putting his arm across my shoulders. It takes time before he can speak.

"Disaster," says Agatha. "The crows fly west."

"I was wrong," Father says, "to think we might be what we are not."

Agatha snorts, and returns to the weaving room.

Mother goes to him and takes his hand. It always warms me to realise that here is more than duty. This is not a marriage neatly arranged for economic reasons. My mother may have been a wife chosen by the family to bring him esteem, but she was also chosen by my father to bring joy within the home. My father is a stranger to the parties where the dancing women tempt, when the men have drunk deep. Here is the love for Father that he deserves.

"What has someone done to make you like this?" asks Mother, leading him to the seat under the vine.

He sits down meekly, a great, handsome man, puzzled, seeking consolation.

"I spoke to a sophist on the matter of Philo becoming his pupil." Father swallows, and steels himself to admit the response.

"He laughed at me. Laughed at me. A sophist, who thinks he is so important. He laughed." Father stares round at us all, looking for our assurance. It is wrong to see a big man so bewildered.

"He said he could not teach the son of a man who would buy knowledge with eggs."

"Rude, for a man paid to teach manners," says Xenia scornfully.

My mother strokes Father's shoulder, giving him strength, but she is too honest to condemn the wise man. Xenia fetches the wine jug and, when she has given a cup to my father, silently hands one to me as well which is not the custom.

What a brief dream has abruptly vanished. But how wise is this man in a clean robe, if he scorns a man such as my father?

# CHAPTER TWO

School days end. Our dreams die with them. Timocrates works at the foundry, bitter with frustration. I
help at the market where Father coughs like a spent
horse. The cough is no longer an extension of his laugh.
The laugh is gone.

"Sometimes I am tempted to acknowledge the gods,"
says Timocrates. "It takes a god to be as cruel as this."

"Do not mock," I plead. "They have power."

"If only they had."

Sometimes I wonder if Timocrates is pleased the
sophist did not like eggs.

Summer is upon us, for the late stars, the Pleiades,
hover in the sky as dawn breaks. This morning I return
home from running in the hills to find Agatha waiting
at the gate. "Your father," she says, animated by a new
development, "has taken to his bed."

Mother comes out of Father's room. Worried as she
looks, and her robe darned, still she has found time to
braid her thick hair high on the back of her head.

"He coughs blood," she says, "and his brow burns,
though he shivers as if the snow is already on the
mountain."

"Blood? That is bad."

"It is worse," says Agatha, but does not elaborate.

"He sleeps now," says Mother, ignoring her. "Philo,
you must tend the stall alone. Some thongs are cut

already. You can work on the rest there. Oh, and there will be some eggs I expect."

"Eggs," says Agatha loudly. "Have you collected the eggs, girl?"

Xenia rummages through the roots of the vine, and peers into the corners of the yard. Her hair bounces angrily around her at Agatha's tart words.

"She has been doing the fire, Agatha. Xenia cannot do everything." I help, looking for eggs in the corner of the weaving room, where the one-eyed hen always lays.

Eventually, loaded with a basket of thongs, another of scones and eggs, scraps of hide under one arm, a knife in my belt, I go. Xenia runs after me and stuffs a piece of bread, spread with honey, into my mouth.

"You get hungry," she whispers, "when you are lonely."

I take time arranging the thongs, putting those of the same length together. Around me the hens screech and pans clatter, while I try to ignore the stench of fish. There are leaves over the eggs to keep them cool. I must resist the temptation to eat Xenia's scones. Blistered hands and the heat are bad enough, but worse is the stink; animals, feet, and dead chickens turning in the sun. The market is quiet without Father's laugh, and his bellow across the stalls.

Already men of affairs are strolling in the colonnade to the south of the market, discussing the business of the city, repeating news that comes in with the boats. And I see the sophists peddling education. I turn my back. Envy destroys.

A small group sits in the shade of a plane tree, around a stocky man whose eyes are like caves hewn out of the rock of his skull. His audience leans forward eagerly to catch his soft voice.

"Cratis. What are the crisis days for pneumonia?" he asks.

The student, Cratis, replies, then tries to stuff the words back among his teeth with his hand. Clearly he gets it wrong.

Bion, the potter, comes across to the stall, needing new thongs for his clay sacks.

"Who is that?" I ask, glancing towards the plane tree.

"Hippocrates."

"Another sophist?"

"A doctor, I have heard. But he does not talk philosophy, or mathematics, or about the stars. Only about medicine. Funny, I say." Bion shakes his head. "No-one is *only* a doctor. Unless you are like him." He points to a gaudy-robed man weaving his way through the groups of people. The colourful creature stares for a moment at Hippocrates, and his tongue darts over his lips, the flicker of a snake. He slips away past a table glinting with fish.

"Silenus, the healer," says Bion, "has more than talk. He has bones and spells, incredible potions. Some say he can do magic in one town, while walking in another."

I daily expect my father to recover and return with me to the market. But he does not. Not even in seven days. Not even in thrice that number.

One day I return to the house, wondering again if he is any better.

"Go to your father, Philo," says Mother, as she prepares soup over the fire.

His eyes are closed, the lids sunk into the deep

shadows beneath his brow. Only now do I realise that the sickness is not of these few days. Father has been ill for as long as he has had that cough.

He lies on the fine couch, our one valuable piece of furniture, but he is not asleep. He opens his eyes and stretches out his hand for me to grasp. The hand shakes a little and is hot to touch.

"There are things I should have given you, Philo. A man should pass on wealth. Position. But I give you less than I received myself. I am ashamed. I am not worthy of our house."

"Stop this talk, Father. You are the finest man in the market place."

"I should not be among the market stalls, Philo, and no more should you." He turns away, and I do not know whether it is sweat or a tear which slides down onto the pillow.

"You have made happiness in the house for Mother and me."

"That is not the same as commanding respect."

Agatha clatters into the room, bearing a dish of soup. "Feeling no better, then?" she says loudly, bumping into the couch. She spills soup down the front of her robe. We help him with his meal, and now he is heavy with sleep.

Agatha returns to the weaving room, and knocks the shuttle against the frame of the loom. I sit down on the wooden seat under the vine and stare before me, seeing not the hens bustling across the yard but myself, standing day after day at the market stall. Now I must cut more thongs for tomorrow. I fetch the knife and a piece of hide and kneel down on the floor to work.

Xenia, without speaking, mocks my slowness as she

grinds corn, rolling the stone backward and forward in the trough so fast that the flour flies everywhere. She smiles at me, determined to lighten my heart.

I keep my head down. Yesterday I did well, having got a large piece of blotchily-stained hide for nothing at the harbour from the man who makes flute bags. I think I will plait some of these thongs for extra strength.

"Xenia."

"Yes?"

"Do you know how ill my father is?"

Xenia sits down beside me, not smiling now. "I have seen."

"He speaks as if...as if...well, could he be wrong?"

"He might be wrong." She takes my hands, staring into my face to exert her will. "Know that nothing happens as we expect it." She sits beside me. She is as good as my sister really.

During the night, Father starts to cough. He coughs until daybreak, and still he gets no relief.

"He wears himself out," says Mother. "We need help."

"Choke to death, I should think," says Agatha.

"Silenus is in town."

"Silenus, yes," says Mother. She pauses only a moment. "Fetch him, Philo."

Silenus, man of magic, colourful as a jay in his striped robe, snakes among the men in white tunics, searching for the ashen cheek, the anxious eye, rattling his bag of magic bones.

"Silenus," I call, dodging after him.

He ignores me. He stares at the men, each so clean with thick fingers like slices of white pig fat. I tap the

magic man's shoulder and wish I had not; the cloak is
tacky with grease.

Silenus looks his client up and down; he notes my
tunic is made of wool, not cotton; marks the frayed
sole of the sandal, and that my hands are leather-
stained.

"My father has need of a healing man." I take a step
back. Silenus smells of sweat and scent, both to excess.

"It will cost silver."

"My mother will pay, but please come."

Ungraciously, Silenus follows me home, his dirty bag
of cures and curios strung from his shoulder, jolting
noisily together. The chickens screech in the yard as
Silenus skates softly to the room where Father lies.
Ignoring Mother, he stands over his patient like a bird
about to peck up a seed from the ground. He glances as
if surprised at Father's couch.

Opening his eyes though dazed with pain, Father
cries out, "You have searched me out too soon, Charon.
I am not ready to come with you." He clings to the
sides of the couch with powerless hands.

"Hush," soothes Mother. She touches his cheek.
"This is not the ferryman; it is Silenus, the healer."

Father lets go of the sides of the couch, and pulls the
blanket up under his chin with fingers grown wiry, but
uncertain these last weeks. He seems smaller within
his own frame, like a nut decayed within its shell.

Silenus touches the cold hand with one finger and
glances at the sweat on the bony forehead.

"I will sell you a prediction." He shakes one of his
bags. "I have bones which speak the truth."

Mother leads him out again into the yard, where the
sun is so bright that even gaudy Silenus looks
bleached. "We want a cure."

"It is too late," he says, with eyes expressionless as a gull's. "Far too late." Turning, he slides out of the yard.

Too late. That is why Father looks like ashes of charcoal, the white cinders of spent fire. Atropos, the third Fate, is at hand to cut the thread.

"Today," Agatha says, "when I tended the fire, I saw good omens in the flames."

"Yesterday, you saw death in the geese flying west," Mother reminds her.

"Best get on weaving a shroud." Agatha nods towards Xenia, busy at the small loom.

Xenia glances at Mother. "This is a new blanket. To be warm against the cold this winter."

"Of course," says Mother. "We work for the future. Oh, Xenia, you understand me as a daughter would."

"Whereas boy children are certain sorrow," Agatha glances at me, and cheers up.

Mother has a new plan. "Catch a fowl, Philo," she says. "We will make a sacrifice."

"At the temple of Demeter?" Mother sacrificed to Demeter to ask for a child to be born to her. Demeter is her proven friend. But she hesitates. "This time to Apollo," she says. "To the shining one, the doctor god."

"Apollo," agrees Agatha. "A goddess is usually better, but we know Demeter has her off-days." She smiles pointedly at me. "I will catch the hen with one eye. It has a shifty look."

"No," says Mother quickly. "Take the hen with the white feather in her wing."

"But she is in full lay."

"I know."

Xenia picks up the doomed hen and strokes its neck. "You are the chosen one," she whispers. "You are set apart from all other hens. Only you will see the great god Apollo cloaked in white light."

"You say there are no gods," I remind her.

"You have to comfort the poor creature somehow."

The temple of Apollo is at the far end of the Sacred Way. Asclepius, son of Apollo, is a god of healing, too, although not an Olympian. Lucky, perhaps, there is no temple to him in the town; losing one hen is bad enough.

The priest kindles the fire on the altar outside the house of Apollo, and ignores me. The breeze carries the fumes towards the temple. I try not to think of the little hen as she used to scuttle round the yard.

The priest takes the chicken away to deal with it in the proper manner; to see that the god receives the best portion. I raise my hands meanwhile to the sky, palms upwards, and standing tall to reach higher, cry, "Oh great Apollo, save my father."

Over my head fly three geese, white and weird, their long necks stretching into the future, their wings flapping lazily, like cloths in the breeze. They are making for the mainland; the geese are flying east.

"Thank you," I whisper. "You have given me a sign."

The sun scorches down on my back. I take the longer road home through the market. The great plane tree by the gate casts its shadows on the cobbles. In its grape-dark shade sits Hippocrates, speaking quietly, filaments of light playing across the rocky face-scape of bone.

If a man is ill, it is wiser to consult a healer like Silenus, or the god or even old Delphia, the herb woman, than it is to consult a doctor with all his talk. But where have I got with Silenus? And why have I chosen the longer route?

Hippocrates pauses. A lizard runs close to his feet. He lifts it up, and directs it among the roots of the plane tree before continuing.

"When a man falls ill, the balance is lost. Only the body can regain its own balance. Our art is to help the body restore harmony. No more than that." He smiles. It is the end of his talk.

Dragging my fingers quickly through my hair, I step forward, pushing past the student called Cratis, who stares, anxious, like a little pale frog having trouble with a gulp. Hippocrates is aware of me and leans forward, expecting a question.

"Please," I say, "please will you come to my father? He is...I think...he is dying."

Hippocrates does not glance about him as Silenus did. "Come. Life is short. Opportunity fleeting."

When we enter the yard, Agatha and Xenia peep out of the weaving room.

"Apollo guided me to him," I whisper to Xenia.

"Rubbish," says Xenia.

Hippocrates looks at my father's pale face with the highly flushed cheeks and strangely sparkling eyes, and at the fingers scratching at the blanket beneath his chin.

The doctor observes him for a long time; he studies every feature.

"You cough blood?" he says at last.

Father nods.

"You sweat in the night, but feel like ice."

"Did Philo tell you?"

"I observe well, my friend."

I notice the doctor's hands. Clean fingers, unlike Silenus, nails cut short, the hands of an aristocrat; the wrists are thick and practical, the wrists of a stone-mason.

"A bath will greatly assist," says Hippocrates.

"I am clean."

"A medical bath. Nothing to do with dirt. I will help."

We drag the hip bath into the room, and start to fill it.

"Something troubles you?"

Father is puzzled that a man in a clean robe should work as a slave. Goodness is not a virtue. Kindness is not its own reward. It adds to his preoccupation with his own standing.

"I am thinking all the time about...Hades. It is fixed in my mind."

"Hades? Why ever do you think of Hades?"

"I am a poor man. As you see from our house, once we had much." He points to the couch. "But my father...and now me...we have grown poor. This is a shameful thing. I have done nothing for my city. Nothing to make other men envy me. I have achieved nothing. I deserve to go to Hades."

"You are not puffed up with pride. You do not influence simple men to your own ends," says Hippocrates, sluicing off the soap with a sponge. "Enough in itself."

"How can it be enough to have sold thongs?"

"Whose shoes do not require thongs?" Hippocrates smiles. "What better work?"

Father half smiles, too.

I watch Hippocrates. It is strange work to do, menial, and yet he has power. A corn merchant has power through money; but the power to wipe away anxiety, no corn merchant's money could buy.

Mother and Hippocrates help Father out of the bath and dry him with a woollen cloth. He starts to cough.

"Whatever now?" says Mother, as he reaches and bends over, struggling for breath.

"The steam is clearing the chest."

We make him comfortable with a clean blanket, and different cushions under his head. He coughs just once more, and I support his chest where the strain falls on the ribs.

"Good," says Hippocrates. "Sleep now. When you wake, take honey water. Boiled, so it sparkles."

The air at last seems cooler, and a goldfinch sings in the vine, *switt-switt*, a happy sound.

Father falls asleep, exhausted by the bath, and the lines of anxiety relax.

Hippocrates leads Mother into the yard. Looking at her gently, his eyes full of pain as if he has taken Father's suffering upon himself, he says, "Nature cannot win this battle."

"But Apollo sent me to find you," I explain.

The doctor shakes his head. "I think not."

"He will not die this season. But the disease cannot be cured. I can tell you the path of the illness. You will come to trust me in this."

"Why are you so certain?"

"Observation. His eyes. Gleam of the skin. Touch. My father taught me this is the only way. Know by what you see. Not by theory."

Mother, proud, stays very calm. "Philo, will you fetch the keys to the chest, please."

"No fee," says Hippocrates. "Since no cure."

Gradually the afternoon fades, while Mother and I sit beside the couch. When Father wakes, Xenia brings a jug of honey water, covered with a small cloth to keep out the flies. She catches my eye to see if I notice how daintily she serves it. She pours a little into a beaker and hands it to me. She seems to know how badly I want to serve my father as Hippocrates served him.

"You feel better already?" says Mother, drawing on her own strength.

"No cure," Father whispers, "but he has given me back myself. I am a man again. I am no longer afraid."

Persephone, daughter of the corn goddess Demeter, returns to Hades each autumn and the swallows are seen no more in the sky.

Timocrates and I meet up in the hills to train. I am so tired, because I stay up late into the night cutting wretched thongs.

"How is the foundry?"

"I hate it. Hate every minute of it. That furnace is like Hades. It spits and roars like a caged animal. It will get me one day. Why should you and I have to live like this?"

"We must pray," I suggest. "Sometimes I think..."

But Timocrates has not changed his mind about the gods.

"The city will send some wealthy weaklings to this summer's games at Delphi." He takes an angry swipe at an offensively spritely dandelion, braving its flowers from the cracked earth. "Delphi will applaud. Poor Delphi, you watch second-best."

"The only way for us, Timocrates, is if the gods..."

"I am the son of an Athenian," says Timocrates. "The gods would favour me, if there *were* gods."

"You will grow strong stoking the furnace at the foundry. I will soon stop selling thongs and eggs, and trade instead with the ships which bring wine from Samos, and gold from Egypt. I will grow rich then."

"Face the truth, Philo. You get the prices wrong, and crack the eggs, and cut uneven thongs which snap."

"Yes, and I cannot go on training, Timocrates. I am so tired. I would not be here now if Xenia had not shaken me awake three times."

Timocrates looks scornfully at me. "I do not give up. Ever. See what I have got here." He dives into some scrubby weeds, and draws out a javelin.

"Where did you get that?"

"Stole it. The only way. I took it from the track, when I was looking for jumping weights there. It was lying in the grass. Forgotten. It is beautiful, look. Shaped to fly higher."

He takes a short run, compresses himself like a spring, and the javelin flies up into the sky, as if to meet Apollo himself in his chariot, breathing, hovering, holding out before dropping to earth in a long, soft arc.

Why look for Apollo in the sky, when he stands here on earth?

My father is alone, and coughing. I go to him, but however I support him, I cannot help him clear his chest. Now I remember he coughs more easily lying on his left side. So I roll him over and sure enough, he finds ease.

I make the cushions more comfortable, and lift the goblet for him to drink.

Hippocrates is at the door, watching.

"You observe well," he says. "No common gift."

He is right. I have learned to see what helps, and what does not, by watching him.

As I dream what I might be doing if not cutting

thongs, less and less do I see myself in the colonnade with a sophist in a white cotton robe. More and more I find myself listening to Hippocrates in the purple shade of the plane tree.

I recognise, eventually, that Lachesis, sister to Atropos, Lachesis, who assigns man's lot, has shown me my fate.

In the grey light of winter, I sit with my father. "Demeter will watch over you, my son," he says, "for you are her gift. I worry now only how you will all live."

"I will provide," I promise, and I think of the thongs, the millions of thongs I might yet have to cut. Lachesis might have shown me my fate, but she has not touched the thread, to make it come about.

I give Father a drink of honeyed water, and bathe his brow. Xenia comes in with her flute and sits playing softly in the ionic key. Father loves her music and falls asleep with a smile on his face.

Inevitably, Persephone returns from the underworld and Demeter, to celebrate, brings green corn to the land once more, pale thin blades, with woodlarks singing above them. As inevitably, Father slips away to another land.

"On the two hundredth day of his illness," says Hippocrates, and places an obol coin in his mouth, to pay for the journey over the River Styx.

All my life, when I remember my father, my thoughts will be of these last days; not of the swaggering man with a laugh, magnified as if by water, but in his days of peaceful self-recognition; I shall remember, always, these warm, salvaged hours.

# CHAPTER THREE

Some days are depressing, scarcely a thong sold; others are better, with money instead of hide to carry home. Today is the best yet.

The island of Cos pays tribute to the city state of Athens in money and in men. In return, Athens keeps the peace for all the city states of the alliance, which some call her empire. It is around this time of the year that the men come home, the cavalry and the foot soldiers, who support the Athenians in their unending quarrel with Sparta, and the oarsmen, who row the Aegean sea, patrolling against pirates and the Persian threat. As the men return, others replace them. It is a profitable time for the armourer and the saddler; it is profitable for a thong maker.

This evening, I sit in the yard, a lamp beside me, cutting tomorrow's supply. What glory in the ambition to sell as many thongs again, all in one day. What an imaginative life stretches before me. I say nothing, although Xenia sits not far away, a small length of cloth in her hands into which she works purple thread.

My mother sits by her, close, as if beside her own daughter. She works on another ribbon, weaving into the cloth a pattern of saffron harebells. Mother makes more ribbons, surely, than she will ever need. Her hands, so strong when they knead bread, are now precise and skilful as she draws threads out to make patterns. From time to time she glances at me with a slight frown as if trying to discern my thoughts.

I try to look happier as I hack away at the hides, try to look as if I do not mind such work.

Agatha patters out of the weaving room and, in the dark, scatters something on the ground on which she spits.

"She has cut her nails," says Xenia.

"Mark how I spit on the pairings, Xenia, so that no-one will work magic against me through them," calls Agatha, and goes with my mother inside the house.

"She is a superstitious old woman," says Xenia. "People should manage their own lives. I will make mine as I want it."

"It is the gods, Xenia." Sounding firm does not make me believe my own words these days.

"You. You only see the trees move," retorts Xenia. "But I see the wind. I see beyond the gods, I see how things truly are."

"The gods punish pride."

"Philo, Philo, do you not see?" Xenia grabs my arm and shakes it with exasperation. "I am not always going to be a slave. Do you think I dare rely on the gods to free me? I shall buy my freedom. I will be as good as any of you one day."

It is true now that she is more nearly my sister than she could ever be a servant. I say, with a surge of generosity, "You are as good as any of us now." It is a mistake.

"I am better," says Xenia. "My ancestors were of the royal tribe."

"You do not know that. You like to think it."

"I know. I feel different. I have never felt like a slave."

"Mother never treats you like a slave, that is why."

"Part of me feels royal all the time."

"Well, it is not your feet."

"Big feet," says Xenia, "are a sign of generosity."

"I wish the gods had bigger feet." What gifts they could so easily bestow; opportunity to learn from Hippocrates; to be chosen for the games; and never to cut another thong.

"I know what *you* want," says Xenia.

"You cannot know."

"You want to be a doctor. I saw the way you watched Hippocrates, watched everything he did."

I shrug.

"You have to make it happen, Philo." She stands before me, so certain and so proud. And so little. It is only her wild hair makes her look taller than she is.

I stand up angrily. "How can I make it happen? I am head of our household. I have to provide for us all. Who else can go to the harbour and bargain for spoiled hides? Who else here has strong enough hands to cut them?"

A breeze rustles through the yard, ruffling the feathers of the sleeping hens. Xenia is staring into space, pretending to see the force that moves the feathers.

"I have sold three hundred thongs today. Think of that. Three hundred stinking, dirty thongs for three hundred stinking, dirty sandals."

I cannot stand the serenity of our yard any longer. The certainty of Xenia and my mother's calm assurance have nothing to do with how I feel.

I run from the yard up the street, and on until I am clear of the houses, until I am panting up the steep hill above the town. These mornings I am too weary to get from my couch before I have to, although I know Timocrates pushes himself every morning up here before facing the hell of the foundry. But now, at this moment, I am bursting with energy, frustrated energy that I cannot use up. I want to run for ever.

I pound over the wiry leaves, the invisible flowers, stumbling on hidden boulders. When I reach the highest point above Astipalea, and all I can see below is the flicker of a lamp in a courtyard, or a soft, amber square of colour, I gather up armsful of grasses and toss them high into the air, so that they shower down over me, seeds clinging to my hair, a trefoil leaf to my lip. I face north, towards where I know great Mount Olympus to be, silent in mist on the mainland, and hold my arms up to the sky.

"See me now, great goddess, see the son of Demeter," I shout. "And think on your work. What reason could there be to make me so poor, yet with great thoughts trapped in my head? Why Demeter, ask yourself, why otherwise did you make me like this?"

I return home slowly, and as I come along the street I see my mother watches for me at the gate. By the time I reach the house, she has disappeared inside.

As I ply my trade, I see, across the market, Timocrates run up to Hippocrates. He cradles his left arm, which is red like a water melon. He curses with pain, glancing at Hippocrates, uncertain.

"No fee." The doctor has taken in the foundry scorches on his tunic. "Bad burn."

"It is not my javelin arm."

"A poultice of grated carrot here, I think."

I watch Hippocrates tend my friend. Medicine is more than making a man well. It is changing his life; giving him a chance.

When the poultice is fixed, Timocrates nods to Hippocrates, and runs off. The doctor stares after him, weighing up his patient.

It is two days later that, as she hands me my evening meal of beans and onions stewed in olive oil, my mother says, "When you have eaten, put on a fresh tunic, Philo."

"This one is no dirtier than usual. The hide was dry today."

She shakes her head. "It has been long on my mind. I realise what you want to do with your life. Philo, you must have your chance. You must go to Hippocrates, and ask him to take you as a pupil."

"How can I do that? I have to work so that we can live. To say nothing of the fee."

"Come." She leads me into the weaving room. The big loom is still. Agatha is no longer shoving the lead through the threads, kicking it if the warp sticks. Like Xenia, she is sitting with small work at the table. Mother points to a basket, which is heaped high with ribbons, braids, bands, filets, nets for the hair, woven with harebell designs, embroidered with shells, bright with saffron and purple, scarlet and emerald.

"Ribbons to sell in the market," says Mother.

"You cannot. I will not let you. It is not seemly."

My mother puts her hands on my shoulders, and these hands are firm and unwavering.

"Why did your father pay for you to go to school? To be a better man than he thought he had been. Would he want you now to command a high fee from the rich, to have the power of holding in your hand a councillor's health? Or would he want you to hack at spoiled hides all day, wearing a dirty tunic as he did?"

"To be a doctor, yes, that is what I want. But not at the price of having my mother sell in the market."

"I saw an owl in the olive tree beyond the wall only this morning," says Agatha. "The sign of Athene. It is a favourable sign."

"You will be the most famous doctor in all the states of Greece," says Xenia. "Philo has cured the councillor's pneumonia. Send for Philo, the general has a stomach cramp. The king of Persia begs that Philo will cure the blisters he got wearing his crown too much."

"It will be for such a short time," says Mother. "And when you can command your fee, we shall be richer than we have ever been. That is what I want."

"It will mostly be me who sells on the market," says Xenia. "Your mother is best at home making more ribbons. Her fingers are nimbler than mine."

"I cannot allow it."

Xenia stands a distance from me, scowling. "I do not know how you can be so stupid, letting us all down like this."

"I *would* be letting you down if I let you sell in the market place."

"It will be me that stands in the market, not your mother."

"Well, you should not either."

Now Mother comes out with the body blow.

"I have sold your father's couch to pay the fee."

"You have done what?"

"It is a fine couch, made for a rich man. Alexander, the merchant, was pleased to buy it from me. He likes fine furniture."

"Father would not have let it go."

"Your father is not here to use it. You have no right to use such a couch until you have proved yourself a fine man, too."

Mother does not raise her eyes from her hands, conscious that her words sound harsh.

I do not know what to say, but Xenia does. She shouts at me,"You great stupid donkey. We have made all those boring ribbons already. The couch is gone for ever. And you have not got enough brain to grasp the opportunity that will help us all."

She stands over me and picks up the dish of vegetables. Quite deliberately, she empties the whole lot over me. "Now you will have to put on a clean robe."

I stare at her, the oil running down my cheeks, the beans making green tracks as they slither down my tunic.

Xenia hesitantly puts her hand up to her mouth. The oil begins to plop off my chin. Xenia struggles to look sorry. She fails and starts to smile.

I look down at the onions on my robe, gliding slowly down oily tracks, and try to scold.

We look at each other, and suddenly we all laugh with relief. I grab Xenia and Mother by the hands, and we leap round the yard, like goats freed from winter shelter.

"Some keep their dignity," sniffs Agatha, and treats herself to a sour smile.

This same evening I go to the home of Hippocrates. The doctor is writing at a table in the courtyard by the light of an oil lamp for the evening is still warm. Behind him, I see into the dining room where the walls are hung with scrolls, more than we ever had at school. I would like to write a scroll that someone would keep hung on a wall. His daughter, with barley-pale hair, slips away when she sees me.

"First thing to learn," he says, without looking up. "Record the day's observations. Make case notes. My father's idea."

"How do you know why I am here?"

"I saw how you tended your father. And I saw your father's couch at the house of Alexander this morning."

"But I am not certain that will provide enough...for the fee," I said. "There might not be..."

"Of course, I charge a vast fee," says Hippocrates, "to rich men. Even larger to stupid men. But to one with compassion but no father, scarcely any fee at all."

"I have compassion."

"An oath," Hippocrates says, without any more preamble, not a man to waste words. "A promise I ask of each student. When better than now?"

He rolls up the papyrus on which he has been writing. "Time has come, Philo, to break free of philosophy. Leave theories hatched in the mind. Put down separate roots as doctors."

"Medicine will be different?"

"Yes. My father knew this. Observation. Forget theories. Disregard superstition."

We are striding through the darkness towards the temple of Apollo. As we pass the last large house before the market place, I see a girl slip through the gate. For a moment I think it is Xenia. Stupid of me. Xenia will be asleep by now. It shows how the excitement of the moment colours the imagination.

"Thinking is not enough, Philo. Observation. I have observed hundreds of cases of pneumonia. I know exactly when a crisis will come. The body itself heals, and we must work with the body. Philosophy cannot tell you that."

Hippocrates seems to look beyond himself, into the darkness, into the future. "A small beginning. We have a vast amount to do."

"Time is short," I repeat his earlier words.

"And knowledge takes a long time to acquire."

Within the house of the god, Hippocrates lights a lamp. We stand together before the table, white marble from Paros, which rests on bandy golden legs. We make an offering of my work which is to come, to the great god of medicine, golden Apollo of so many gifts.

How strange it is that the fortunes of my two ambitions lie in the hands of the same god. This should help me.

"I swear by Apollo the healer," says Hippocrates.

"I swear by Apollo the healer," I repeat after him, and go on repeating after Hippocrates, "and by Asclepius, to use my power to heal as well as I am able; I will not harm any person through this art, I will not give poison if I am asked, nor give a woman the means to procure an abortion. I will not perform operations until I am truly skilled. Finally, I will hand on my knowledge to none but sworn pupils."

We stand for a moment in the yellow light of the small lamp, as if bathed in the benevolence of Apollo himself. But for me, there is more than the oilwick light, there is a power from somewhere beyond the gods, a power which resides in Hippocrates, a power which will one day be mine. Will I then be Apollo's child? At last, the thread of my life is racing on the spindle. Demeter has heard my prayer, and had a word with Clotho, sister to Lachesis, Clotho who spins the thread of life, and told her to get on with it.

# CHAPTER FOUR

There are eight in the medical school, as Hippocrates calls us, but most of the others have much experience. Only Cratis and Nicodemus are little wiser than I, and we fall together as each day we make a round of the patients.

"Delphia," says Hippocrates, "lies at the house of a crone near the city gate. She has a leg wound."

I have not seen Delphia, the old herb woman, in the market recently, shuffling from one patch of shade to the next, baskets spilling lovage and gnarled roots and fennel around her.

"Sulking. Because I insist no poppy be sold for pleasure." Hippocrates walks briskly.

"Do you not think she is a peculiar woman?" Cratis scuttles to keep up.

"No. And we need Delphia."

"She is a disgusting old hag," yawns Nicodemus, untroubled as a cat. He looks born to be among the privileged who haunt the colonnade, instead of with Cratis and me.

An aura hangs over Delphia, a smell of stewed onions combined with scant familiarity with the wash bowl. She lies on a couch, her leg inflamed and bound in dirty rags.

"Hippocrati," she says, sensing a small victory. "You don't want to lose me, seeing as I know so many more things than you."

"You know wrong things."

"I could try your new-fangly cures," she says grudgingly, "though where the plants fail me, you won't win. To the plants of old Delphi you'll turn again."

"What happened here?" Hippocrates unwinds the strip of rag.

"In the Dikeos mountains, I go looking for bearberry. You'll not pick that in Astipali. As if you'd know that." She gives a thin spit to show contempt. "These things are left to old Delphi. What did I do but stumble over an old black rock and tear my leg apart."

She gapes down at the curdled gash. Nicodemus moves to the end of the palliasse and puts his hand in front of his nose.

Delphia smirks up at him. "You're a fine man to be in this place," she says. "Gone tumble down in the world, have you?"

Nicodemus ignores her. "Is there no-one else who can cut roots?"

Hippocrates pauses. "Not like Delphia."

"You and me knows that," says Delphia, digging her elbow into the doctor's side. Nicodemus smiles when Hippocrates steps back.

"Observe," says Hippocrates, "the colour of the pus. Dark. Not good. Leg hot, is it?"

Cratis makes notes on the hem of his tunic. He carries a fragment of charred stick for the purpose.

"D'you know," gulps Delphia, "but I filled it with thorns, as I slithered down the slope. I heard the spirits laughing, jealous as you'd guess. Jealous that old Delphi knows more than they. And now we go rotten."

"Yellow matter absorbs poison. Nature's way. You have tried some of your herbs, I suppose?"

"Coltsfoot."

"And?"

"Sage. Comfrey. Garlic."

Cratis is running out of hem.

"No more, surely."

"Marshmallow. Pellitory-of-the-wall. Couchgrass. Black hellebore."

"Why a purge?"

"Didn't work neither. Nor did poppy help poor Delphi's pain."

"So, now my art."

"A bit of funny doctoring," agrees Delphia rather grudgingly.

I learn how to clean a wound with wool and wine, holding my breath as I work.

"You'll do no good with that," advises Delphia.

Hippocrates plasters it with wax, softened with oil.

"Muck, I'd say."

"Bandage please, Cratis."

Cratis is meticulous, covering the whole leg, and the pattern is ornate. He uses a great deal of bandage and takes an age.

"Too much of a good thing," says Hippocrates. "Delphia, keep it clean." Turning to the old crone standing by, he says, "Delphia has a fever. Only honey water to drink. Thin gruel when fever goes."

"Starvation won't do no good. No more that fancy bandaging," says Delphia, grimacing to show the black gaps in her teeth.

Meanwhile my mother weaves ribbons, and the skill is not only in her fingers, but in her mind; for out of imagination, she plucks lilies, and swags of laurel, and little blue singing birds which have never been seen, and weaves them into her ribbons.

But now, her busy hands still, she stares at the white walls as if she is seeing something quite different.

"Are you so very tired, Mother?"

She smiles wistfully at me. "I am not tired, Philo, but I like sometimes to dream." She looks down at her ribbon and starts to work again. "To remember how things were."

"You loved my father."

"I am grateful to remember; not bitter to think of the loss. It is given to very few women to love their husbands. A father might choose carefully for his child in marriage, but how can he make certain there will be love?"

"Will I be lucky, Mother?"

"I pray for it, Philo, every time that I pray to Demeter for your happiness."

I smile, but I would prefer my mother to turn in her heart to Apollo. For one thing a man god would be wiser in such matters.

Agatha makes fewer ribbons and all plain because she cannot be inconvenienced with decoration. Xenia goes every day to the table in the market where Father once sold thongs, and stays until enough have been sold to buy corn for bread and wool to weave.

I know they hate it, but no-one complains. In fact, Xenia gets up early. I hear her singing noisily as she crosses the yard. I imagine she is working even then on more ribbons.

But I am wrong, because this afternoon I return to find her waiting for me, hands behind her back.

"You never thought of this," she announces triumphantly.

"What has genius thought up now?"

46

"Look."

Restless with pleasure, she hands me a woven bag. Grabbing it back, she opens it out flat to reveal ten pockets.

"Like Hippocrates has," she says. "A doctor's bag. The narrow pockets are for knives, and the rest for medicines."

I go to hug her, but hesitate. For some reason, Xenia is not quite so like a sister as she once seemed.

"Why not get some bones, and go round the island like Silenus?" says Agatha. "People say he has a hoard of coins stored away."

"Silenus is not a worthy man," says Mother.

"I do not see what is worthy about sitting under a tree all day," says Agatha.

"The bag is perfect, Xenia. You do so much for me." She bounces away, embarrassed by her own generosity.

Nicodemus is in his courtyard, surrounded by a great deal of wood. Hippocrates and I walk by on our way to the market place.

He stands up, radiates his easy smile. "I am sorry. I did not behave well to Delphia. I should have hidden my revulsion."

"Towards an inferior?" asks Hippocrates.

Nicodemus laughs. "Come Hippocrates. Delphia stank like a hog. You even shrank away yourself when she touched you."

"She offended my nostrils. Not the same thing." He picks up a piece of wood.

"What do you think of this?" Nicodemus is making a bed of sorts, but with bars across either end.

"Remember the fractured thigh we set three days

ago, how difficult it was? With this, we can get lever-
age to line up the bones."

"Mmm." Hippocrates nods. "That case is not healing. He moves too much."

"Then you could tie him to this bed," says
Nicodemus, "until the bones are set. Uncomfortable,
of course."

"Clever. Hard on the patient."

"You think I lack compassion?"

"Not careless with it, Nicodemus."

There comes the sound of a child from within a
room.

"I guard against sentimentality. Even where my son
is concerned." He glances towards the house. "It is not
good to be soft. And not easy to be hard with Menon.
Extraordinary child."

"How old is he?" I ask.

"Fifteen months. But his mind. He will be a credit to
me. Only yesterday he discovered what made his pottery pig rattle. He is young to show such curiosity. He
cracked it open on the floor; heart broken when he
found the rattle was made by five little pottery balls
inside the pig."

"No rattle. No pig."

"Knowledge is pain, Hippocrates."


Later in the day we are told Maco, the lyre maker, has
broken his nose in a fight.

"You know the bandage, Cratis?" asks Hippocrates.

"I know exactly. I have written down all the bandages. This is up and round the left ear. Across and
under the chin. So."

"Surely that is for the jaw." Nicodemus tilts his head
back, and his nose appears more privileged than ever.

Cratis frowns. "Leave it to me." He goes off, bandaging an invisible head.

We reach the market when Timocrates walks by, delivering goods. He sees me. I feel his envy. He says, quiet with scorn, "No need to run in the hills now, is there?"

"I am sorry, Timocrates."

"How did you get in with him, Philo?"

"I think he noticed the way I cared for my father."

He glances at me. "I would do anything to be in your place. Anything."

At home, I practise my art, writing notes about the patients seen that day. Medicine must observe fact, not invent theories to explain sickness. I note the crisis days of the pneumonia patients, and the gruel diet for the fever cases.

But the practical art of bandaging is more elusive. I practise on a table leg, spiralling away.

Xenia stops grinding corn and erupts into the weaving room. "You can bandage my ankle if you like."

"You will be impressed."

She sits on the table, and holds up her left foot. There is a strange fragrance, like flowers, but like spice, too.

Xenia has rubbed the foot with perfumed oil before offering to let me bandage it. The other is still dry and dusty.

"I can only bandage a right foot."

Annoyed, Xenia tosses her head. "I cannot afford to splash perfumed oil about like chicken grain. I am saving up."

"Saving up for what?"

"My freedom."

"What are you saving up?"

"The money I earn. Oh." She puts her hand over her mouth.

"What money?"

Xenia drops her head. She has said more than she intended. I suddenly realise I did see her the night I swore the doctor's oath.

"I play the flute. At men's parties."

"You play the flute, where?" I ask. I heard the answer. I hoped it might come out different.

Xenia looks stubbornly at the ground.

"So you creep out of the house when we think you have gone to bed?"

"I have talent, and they pay me well."

"But Xenia, the flute girls are often more than musicians. That is no way to earn money."

Xenia laughs. "I only play the flute. I am respected. But how else can I ever buy my freedom?"

"You must be careful, Xenia."

"Do not worry. Drunk as Dionysus, most of them. I leave early and run home."

"What difference will it make to be free? We would treat you the same. You are like a sister to me now, and a daughter to Mother."

"As a slave, I can marry only into slavery, and my children will be born slaves. If I can free myself, and marry a free man, my children will be free as birds."

"How much must you save up?"

"I do not know exactly for what your mother would sell me, but whatever that is, I shall save it up. Even if it takes me ten thousand days."

"It will take me as long to be a doctor, I expect."

"Anything new is hard, Philo. But you will do well, I

know it. Because you care about everything so much."

Xenia waggles her foot just a little; the smell of jasmine creeps up my nose.

"Keep still." I glance up, and she is looking down at me.

I see that like all women of Persia before her, she has lashes that are longer than necessary merely to trap dust.

Xenia is two years younger than I, she always will be. But her eyes know of matters that are older than us both.

"You are cured," I tell her lightly, and unwind the bandage. Because I am no longer a child, I bow to her mockingly, looking directly into her eyes until she glances away. I have no intention of being intimidated by whatever it is that Xenia knows, and which I do not understand at all.

In the evening, we make a second visit to a man with pneumonia. He is in the critical fourth day of his illness. He has pulled through, and we are relieved he is safe until the seventh day now. We walk home in the fading light.

"What is that?" whispers Nicodemus.

At the end of the street is a ghostly white sphere, floating unevenly from one side of the road to the other, some way above the ground. It collides with a wall, and rebounds, as if offended.

"An ancestor," murmurs Nicodemus, "returned from the house of Hades."

The white sphere plummets to the ground. After a moment it rises up again, slowly and uncertainly, before meandering on its way to meet us.

"We could go this way." I point up a side street. But

coming out of the side street is Cratis, looking into each gateway as he approaches.

"I have mislaid a patient."

"A bandage," says Nicodemus. "It is a bandage, some idiot's work." Sure enough, the white sphere is a man's head totally encased in an abundance of woollen strips. No mouth to be seen, no nose, no eyes. In the dark, his black cloak has concealed his body.

"Maco?" says Cratis. His expression alternates between pride and doubt. "This is Maco. And my bandage, too."

"*Clumph*," says Maco, hearing his name.

"Is it all right?" asks Cratis, spitting a little. "The bandage? It took me the whole afternoon."

Delphia's wound is no better. She glares triumphantly at my puzzled face. "Done no better than old Delphi," she croaks. "Not so well, I'd say."

She looks odder than usual. Her filthy hair is tied up in a ribbon. By its wayward embroidery, I recognise Xenia's work.

"Where did you get the ribbon?"

"Business."

"Did Xenia give it to you?"

"Business."

What does Xenia want of Delphia? Not belladonna, I hope, to drop in her eyes and make them lustrous, as do the women of light love. No, of course Xenia would do nothing of the kind, but I must ask her exactly how Delphia came by those ribbons.

"What a mess," says Cratis. "We must do something."

In our courtyard Xenia is on her knees in the corner,

scrabbling at the ground with a weaving shuttle, using it to dig.

"Go away," she says, "until I have finished. This is a surprise."

"What did Delphia give you?"

"Oh. So you know." She stops teasing, looking disappointed.

"It was to be a surprise." She points to a plate beside her. "Until they start to grow."

On the plate are seven small heaps of seeds, each a different shape and colour.

"A herb garden. Not just the sage and chives we grow for cooking, but medical plants that Delphia knows about. I gave her three ribbons for these."

I stand above her feeling clumsy; I have spoiled her gift. "I cannot keep up with your ideas, Xenia."

"One day you will catch up." She scatters the seeds on the earth, with a swaying motion, like a seed head stirring in the wind, so that they fall into irregular patches. Strange girl, I would have sown them in rows.

Being a student of medicine is not all work. Most men race and wrestle or throw the javelin to grow beautiful in body and to find fame. But Hippocrates brings us to the track, or the palaestra, most days after work because it makes us healthy.

This afternoon, we race on the track; as usual I am in the lead after the turn, though I can hear Nicodemus behind me. He never seems to try, but covers the track like an antelope with huge, earth-eating strides.

We sprint a two-length race, and as we pelt back towards the starting sills I see Timocrates standing there, looking serious. I strive harder, to avoid his scorn. I am not certain of his mood. Jealousy is a tenacious friend.

But Timocrates smiles, almost nervously.

"Not injured again?"

"Not this time. I want to speak with Hippocrates."

"He is talking. Over there. In the shade."

"Come with me, Philo, and hear what I ask him."

Hippocrates does not look surprised to see Timocrates.

"The man who does well with a javelin." He smiles.

"Could you do with another student?" Timocrates comes straight out with it. No preparing the way.

"Depends on the student."

"I can pay my fee," says Timocrates and holds up a bag.

It is bulging. How can he ever have saved that money?

"To be a doctor?" muses Hippocrates, not impressed with the money.

Timocrates nods.

"Or to run in the stadium?" asks Hippocrates.

Timocrates hesitates. "Bit of both."

"Not good enough," says Hippocrates quietly, and turns away as if there is no more to say. But he looks again at Timocrates from his deep-set eyes, and there is a question there like an invitation to speak again.

Timocrates swallows. "I have written this." He hauls from his pouch a tattered papyrus, and glances at me to see if I approve.

"Yes?" The voice is encouraging.

"If you could keep completely healthy, you would avoid much illness."

"Continue."

"I have written it down, see? How you need to drink more in the summer, and eat different food in the winter. And if you run before you eat, you get thinner."

He watches anxiously while Hippocrates reads the regime.

Eventually the doctor smiles. "Excellent observation. Also a topic I hold dear. We will study together."

Timocrates can only go for a triumphal gallop down the track, leaping like an elk among the crags.

"You will not be disappointed," I say, pleased for my friend.

"How else," asks Hippocrates, "will he train for Olympia?"

Later, we walk home together. "How will you live, Timocrates, until you can ask your own fee?"

"I have the money."

"Not your mother's..."

"The necklace. It is sold."

"It is really valuable, then? Far more valuable than my father's couch?"

"Gold," says Timocrates, "and the stones were emeralds, every one."

"Why did your mother decide to sell it now?"

Timocrates stares beyond me to the hills above the town. "It is sold," he repeats.

Delphia's wound is more inflamed. Nicodemus looks down his nose but says nothing. Her bandages are carelessly wound on her leg, and she has on a dressing of walnut juice.

Delphia leers up at me. "It's your plan," she pipes. "I knows. While old Delphi fades, you look for her silver. You won't find old Delphi's silver, not any of you."

"Rubbish. The bandages have been tampered with," I note suspiciously.

"I like to watch how it's getting along."

"It is not getting along at all with you interfering."

"Leave her to me," says Nicodemus. "She is a stubborn old woman. But I have the matter in hand."

"And you're a sly rogue," says Delphia, pleased. "I shan't die. It's a wonder I'm still here after all this doctoring."

"Quiet, woman."

"Sheep's gut," says Delphia, "is one answer." She leans over to the cooking pot on the table, and slaps a piece of foul-smelling meat on the wound.

"Get your dirty hands out of the way, Delphia. I shall apply a yarrow poultice."

"That's a tame little weed. You want a plant with a bit of power to it."

"I am the doctor. You are the patient." He moves all her herbs out of reach. Delphia shrugs and stares resentfully at the bandages.

There is a clatter outside the door and Timocrates and Cratis appear, carrying the bed that Nicodemus designed for fracture cases.

"Firewood?" asks Delphia, surprised. "Kindling for Delphi?"

"Take her feet, Cratis." Nicodemus gets hold of Delphia under the arms. "Heave her over."

"Put me back," shrieks Delphia.

"Strap her on firmly," instructs Nicodemus. "And you only come off that when there is one of us here."

In four days the wound is healed and Hippocrates inspects the new, clean skin. "Excellent."

"Such cruelty, Hippocrati. That one's a rogue."

"Cured your leg, though."

"What? It was my own yarrow that sewed me up. My

own herbs, you mark that, Hippocrati, and don't you come asking no fee."

Cratis murmurs, "Yarrow." And commits it to the hem of his robe.

"To the herbs of old Delphi you turns." She cackles, hobbling past Nicodemus, flapping her arms like a fowl.

# CHAPTER FIVE

Timocrates scorns my laziness as the time of testing draws near. "Come to the stadium for some serious practice."

I have not trained at all recently, doing only what other men do, run for fun, or wrestle a little most afternoons. Medicine has evicted my earlier dream.

"We train for the foot race, twenty-four lengths."

"Why not a two-length sprint?"

"The foot race is my event." Timocrates thinks not of me, only of my benefit to him as competition.

We each cover the white sand well, but Timocrates finishes ahead.

Near the sills stands a man whom I recognise instantly by his fine robe and majestic bearing. The Archon, state officer of our town, a man who makes decisions. Timocrates sits on the ground, getting his breath, and the Archon saunters over.

"Do I know your name, young man?"

Timocrates hurries to his feet, as if stung by a hornet.

"Timocrates." There is no trace of his usual disdain.

The Archon nods, saying nothing. He strolls off, clearly puzzled. He must think he knew all the rich men's sons who spend their afternoons training on the track.

But he turns and walks back, staring at Timocrates with eyes narrowed in concentration. "Have I also seen you throw the javelin?"

"Yes. As far as the fifth cypress tree."

As the Archon nods again and goes away, Timocrates punches my shoulder, and his laugh is a snarl of joy.

We scrape our bodies clean in the bath house, where Nicodemus argues with a patient who defected to the Asclepium, the place of healing built around the temple of Asclepius at the far end of the island.

"There was smoke," says Cleon, "smoke, and a glow from the inner room like phosphorus on the sea. The priestess said, 'The signs are good.' She said that to me. The words echoed round the walls like the thunder of Zeus. And I am cured."

"The signs *were* good all the time," says Nicodemus, almost ruffled. "*We* said you would recover. You are a fool." He scorns Cleon, who moves to another group to repeat the tale of his miraculous cure.

"Faith. Superstition. Neither are medicine," murmurs Nicodemus. "A trick. 'The signs are good.' That could mean anything. Passes for truth. The Asclepium is spurious."

"The power of brevity," Hippocrates points out. "The aphorism. Tell me about empyema, Cratis."

"Empyema which empties slowly, heals quickly," says Cratis. "I remember you saying that yesterday."

"Precisely. What are you doing?"

"Writing it down."

"The point of an aphorism is that it is easy to remember." Nicodemus turns his scorn on Cratis. "And you write it down."

"I like to have a record," says Cratis. "Heals... quickly."

We visit Medea, a woman much troubled by scaly skin. Cratis clutches a poultice of purple loosestrife he is convinced will cure her. Her small white house stands at the edge of the town.

"Where is the patient?" asks Hippocrates of an old woman at the yard door.

The woman hesitates. "You cannot. She is...she is sleeping."

"Tell her we have some new medicine for her," says Cratis.

"No," says the woman firmly. "She cannot see anyone."

"Waste of time. The patient must want to be cured." Nicodemus bounds away. "What patients we have. Cleon with his humbug at the Asclepium, and now Medea being coy."

A chance to see the Asclepium for myself comes quickly. A message arrives from the temple of healing near the village of Chora that Theodorus, the chief priest, is ill. The message comes not from him, but Hicetas, his deputy.

We arrive at the pillared gateway; Hicetas, a tall man with a nervous smile, meets us. It is evening, for the Asclepium is the best part of a day's ride across the island. We have borrowed donkeys, but they are so clumsy that however hard I try, I cannot imagine it is a horse.

"Hippocrates," says Hicetas, "welcome."

"A pleasure." Hippocrates clasps his shoulders. "Shall we see our patient, Theodorus, immediately?"

Nicodemus is smiling as we walk across the courtyard.

We enter the sick priest's cell-like room to hear a

cough, rattling and unproductive. Theodorus is grey-faced on his couch, scarcely able to smile when he sees Hippocrates.

"I did not send for you," he whispers. "I believe we can find our own cure."

"You feel hot?" Hippocrates wastes no time.

"It is the weather."

"Weather is quite cool. You have a temperature, Theodorus. It is at least pneumonia, as you must know."

Theodorus lies on the couch, breathing like a cow in labour, wincing with pain.

"And the Asclepium has no cure?" Nicodemus mocks.

"Hush," Cratis tells him and smiles politely at Hicetas, overawed by the religious aura.

"It is the invisible dagger in his side. It will kill him. It turns with every breath," whispers Hicetas. "It defies the priestess, Aspasia."

"What has been done?"

"Everything. Aspasia has left nothing untried."

We observe his face, his eyes, touch his brow, listen to his breathing, note the fingers, enquire the days of high fever.

I know it is more than pneumonia. "Lung abscess?"

"Possible. First we try to clear the lungs. Honey and vinegar – warm. Small sips. We note any change in the morning. Act accordingly."

As we leave the cell, a small procession approaches, led by a priest. A woman enveloped in a dark cloak follows, carrying an alabaster flask of oil, a gift for the god. She walks with her head down, but the gift thrust high before her. Behind her, a man wobbles beneath a tray of unruly honey cakes.

One falls off the tray, and Timocrates swoops down upon it.

"She has already been purified by the priest," explains Hicetas. "A three-day ritual. And now she will be allowed to go into the temple and make her offering. Aspasia will decree her treatment. She will sleep in a specially prepared room. If fortunate, the healing snakes will come to her, perhaps in a dream."

"The three-day purification," says Nicodemus. "Is that to confuse the patient?" He looks at Hicetas in the manner of a magistrate.

Hicetas smiles at Nicodemus as if to scold him. "Our patients are frequently confused already."

The procession comes closer. The hood of the cloak partly screens the woman's face. But not completely.

"So," says Nicodemus.

The woman glances up, causing the hood to fall back.

Nicodemus steps forward. "Medea," he says. "So this is why we could not see you at your house."

Medea hesitates. One cheek is gaudy with her rash, yet flecked with pale, dry scales.

"I had some very nice purple loosestrife," says Cratis.

"Aspasia waits," says Hicetas briskly, realising he has taken one of Hippocrates' patients. That wipes the smile off his face. He knows he has broken the code of courtesy that exists between us.

"I will show you the rooms I have prepared," says Hicetas. "I am afraid there are only two for the five of you, but we have so many patients here now." He smiles, and leaves us.

The rooms, where usually a patient will sleep in the hope of healing dreams, are small. So are the bowls of dried fish which provide a token supper.

Hippocrates lingers in the fragrant darkness. "An aspect to the east is always healthy. No conflicting winds." With a sigh, he admits, "I want this place. Rooms to teach. Rooms to operate. A home for the medical school. Medicine would break free from philosophy, from unscientific arts."

"They should welcome us," says Cratis. "Teach them medicine instead of all this superstitious nonsense."

"They would not have us. And we must be with the people." Hippocrates looks wistfully out onto the night from his deep, brooding eyes. "Asclepius. God of medicine," he murmurs.

"Who *was* Asclepius?" asks Cratis, trying hard to remember.

"Son of Apollo, who took him from his mother Coronis at birth. Gave him to the wise centaur, Chiron, who taught him the powers of plants on Mount Pelion. See, Chiron is above us, and the archer Sagittarius." He points to the stars.

Cratis draws a star map in the air.

"Here our name would live for ever." Hippocrates goes into a room, lost in his own thoughts.

I am ebbing into sleep, when Nicodemus whispers loudly, "Come with me."

I am outside the door before asking, "What are we doing?"

"We must discover their secret. I am certain the priests are not what they seem."

"Why me?"

"Would Hippocrates come with me?"

"I see."

"This next room, I think, is a pharmacy. I noticed priests coming and going with small flasks." He opens the door. "Yes, it is."

"Great Zeus."

The room is lit by a lamp. On shelves round the walls are jars, their smells boasting spices, alien and exotic. Here are cups, ready with liquids, thick and bright, and sheaves of leaves rustling above our heads.

"Never seen the like," mutters Nicodemus. "These must come from the Ganges, or from Egypt. Roots from the East. Leaves from Macedonia."

"Here is monkshood. Surely that is thornapple."

"You are right, Philo. All plants we would never use. All these give hallucinations. So that is how it is done."

"Are you satisfied now? Can we go back to bed?"

"One more place I must see. The temple. Aspasia presides at night. She can create a stranger light."

"We cannot go in there, Nicodemus."

"Of course we can."

We creep up to the higher level, where the temple gleams white against the forest, the enchanted forest, where no man ever dies, nor any has ever been born. I watch the last patient go inside. Nicodemus approaches the entrance. I straggle behind.

The priest accompanying a patient in front has a bit of trouble getting him to walk out and Nicodemus limps in, unremarked.

Aspasia stands behind the table in a weird green light. "My one leg is shorter than the other," whines Nicodemus.

Aspasia rolls up her eyes. Then she gurgles and rumbles.

This is the message of the god coming through,

I suppose.

In a voice distant with wisdom, Aspasia says, "Your leg will grow a little yet." She avoids specific limbs.

Nicodemus smiles. His arrogant leer remains as he walks jauntily out of the temple, without any limp at all. At the door he turns and waves to her.

"Now they know we have found them out, they will give us no trouble." Nicodemus strides back to our room.

We are woken early with a meal of vegetables fresh from the field below the wall. The small onions and beans stewed in oil taste good, but lavish they are not.

"Excellent." Timocrates looks round hopefully. He eyes the other priests, all thin, like white furled flags on slender poles. I know what he is thinking.

Theodorus is worse, meandering into unconsciousness. He lies is an unnatural position to protect against pain.

"It is a lung abscess?" I ask again.

Hippocrates nods. "You know what to do?"

"Bring me bran and vinegar, two sacks of fine cloth, some thread in a needle. And stoke up the oven," I tell Hicetas.

Theodorus reacts to my voice, staring with fear.

"The pain is there?" I touch the left ribs.

The priest tries to concentrate. He nods.

"It is a lung abscess. The pus must drain and then the pain will go."

Theodorus stares at me, trying to focus. "Not the knife," he whispers. "Do not cut me with the knife. Always, we have faith in other methods."

"I, also, have another method."

Into the bran goes the vinegar, making a moist blend

to pack into the two sacks, which I sew up like plump hen birds.

"Heat in the oven for as long as it would take to walk to Chora."

I turn Theodorus to lie on his right side. He sweats and screams out with every move, eyes rolling up under the lids.

Now he lies more quietly, but I do not trust the calm. He is losing consciousness, and the fever rages. Atropos, who cuts the thread, is close.

When the bran bags come back, warm from the oven, I hold them either side of the priest's chest. The colour from the moist bran stains his white robe even before the heat-retaining blanket covers him.

"Now we must wait."

"You will do no good," says Hicetas. "I should have had faith in our own powers."

"It is within our power," says Hippocrates.

We wait.

The bags are reheated.

Still we wait.

"The time is not yet," says Hippocrates.

The breathing is worse.

"You can do nothing," says Hicetas. There is the hint of a smile. He is, after all, the deputy chief priest.

"We try again," I tell him. "Only this can help. We must make the heat work with the heat of the body to fight the disease."

So more hot bran bags, and the reek of vinegar in our nostrils. Theodorus loses consciousness again.

Just before noon comes a strange crackling sound from deep within Theodorus' chest. He starts from his unconscious sleep to cough without restraint.

"This is the end," cries Hicetas.

"No," I shout triumphantly, and we watch the evil matter of the abscess splatter all over the blanket.

I look at Hippocrates and he watches me, not the patient. For the first time, we share the same power. I have defeated Atropos, I have steered fate. He nods, understanding. Am I now Apollo's child?

Theodorus lies back, focussing, wide-eyed, on me. "The pain. It is gone. I can breathe again."

"So you triumph," says Hicetas.

Hippocrates says, "We will make a sacrifice to Asclepius, our inspiration. May we also pay our respects to Aspasia?"

The smoke from the altar rises into the clear, ringing air, while the smell of the cockerel on the fire causes Timocrates to swallow hard.

Hippocrates carries a small silver statue of an athlete, an image of health, which he intends to lay on the table of the god, a gift to Asclepius. We wait for Hicetas to tell us that the priestess, Aspasia, is ready to see us.

"That young woman is an impostor," Nicodemus tells Hippocrates.

"How do you know she is young?"

"Because I saw her."

"When?"

"Last night."

At last the priest appears. He looks worried. "I am afraid Aspasia will not see you," he says. "She will not be persuaded. In fact, she does not attend the temple. She sleeps."

"No surprise," says Nicodemus.

"You have made an enemy," Hippocrates tells him.

"She must be tired," he continues tactfully. "I will still make my gift to the god."

"Of course," says Hicetas, knowing that the silver statue will go into their coffers.

Hippocrates lays the offering on the temple table. The silver figurine is beautiful, and perhaps the artist had Timocrates in mind when he made the mould.

We stand for a moment, and the silence of the temple holds the breath of the great god. Suddenly, a deep voice booms through the vents, which are cunningly constructed to add mystery to the voice of the priestess beyond.

"Thank you, oh great doctor."

The priest flinches. This is not the voice of Aspasia for certain. It is rare and powerful. Who else would speak from the inner room but the great Asclepius himself? The god has come to his house. Hicetas prostrates himself on the floor.

"Hicetas," comes the voice again. "Flatter the healing men with rich food."

I glance round. Timocrates is missing. Hippocrates strides swiftly outside, unnoticed by Hicetas, who is too busy knocking his head on the ground.

Through the vents comes the unmistakable sound of crunching. I clatter my sandals on the floor to cover the sound.

Then a door slams.

We help the shaken Hicetas to his feet.

"That happen often?" asks Cratis stupidly.

We go into the sunshine to meet Hippocrates with a subdued Timocrates. Unwillingly, I realise what he has done now. He has raided the store of food, which is sacred to the god, eaten honey cakes which were gifts from patients. Crumbs still cling to his chin.

"Mocking the gods is a crime. Punishable by death," says Hippocrates, as we return.

"I was starved. And I kept thinking of all those cakes that must be in the room behind the altar. Anyway, the gods never hear my prayers, so they will not hear my joke."

"Hubris lies not in one action, Timocrates. You will be punished for believing yourself equal."

Nicodemus *has* made an enemy. Medea returns home with stories especially given to her by Aspasia; tales of patients by name that Hippocrates has failed to cure. Patients who have become worse with treatment. Patients who have died, including my father.

"I will speak with Medea," says Nicodemus. "I shall tell her what happened when *I* met Aspasia. She might welcome our treatment now. I favour marigold for eczema."

I go with him, sensing victory.

"I wish to see Medea," says Nicodemus, with the authority that comes naturally to him.

"Certainly," says the old woman who stands before us. "There she is, see?"

Medea steps from the weaving room into the courtyard.

The marigold drops from Nicodemus' hand.

Her skin is as smooth as a healthy apple; not a flake, nor sore, nor rash to be seen. The Asclepium has given her spiritual peace, and she is healed. She smiles at us, then turns slowly and goes inside.

# CHAPTER SIX

In the spring, two visitors come to Astipalea. One is the three-day fever, rarely serious, but prolific. Hippocrates favours natural recovery. The fever is less dangerous than the second intruder.

"There is a stranger in the town," Timocrates says, "calling himself a doctor. I saw him in the market place, touting for patients."

"What is his name?" asks Hippocrates.

"Euryphon."

"Euryphon. You come at last."

"You know him?" asks Nicodemus.

"I do."

"A rogue, like Silenus?"

"A successful doctor of the Cnidus school; successful, but a bad doctor. Patients enjoy his unctuous manner."

"Rivals." Cratis thinks he understands.

"No doctor is a rival," Hippocrates tells him. "The Cnidus school I deplore, although they, too, recognise medicine is an art separate from philosophy. Impressive manner; no observation. Talk. Talk does not cure."

"Does it matter Euryphon is here?" asks Nicodemus.

"A nobody?"

"He comes to humiliate my method."

Euryphon, elegant, watches the merchants under the colonnade. Nearer, behind the sandal stall, a small, dirty old woman darts away, limping a little.

"Delphia," Hippocrates calls. "I have seen you."

Slowly, the old crone approaches us, as if by chance.

"You run away from me, Delphia. Usually so anxious to sell your herbs."

"You forget I cured you," Nicodemus reminds her coldly.

"I've no herbs today, good doctor," she says softly, her shifty eyes darting across his face.

"I need yarrow, Delphia," says Hippocrates. "Dried leaves. Also some fenugreek plants. My own are gone."

"I'll search for them," she says meekly, cowed like a dog which has been hit, but without a dog's respect.

"Delphia, you old rogue," says Hippocrates, "what is the matter? Herbs are in your basket."

"Spoken for," says Delphia stubbornly.

"Told you before, old woman, sell only to the doctors. Not to those without the art. They overdose."

"A man who glimmers Atropos at the window will pay big," says Delphia and laughs to herself.

"They die, Delphia. I am always here."

She grimaces up to him with what she believes is a winning smile.

"Wicked old woman, Delphia, but clever. You will find the yarrow?"

"Tomorrow, Hippocrati. Trust old Delphi. Be a drachmi more."

"Delphia," says Hippocrates.

She shrugs her bony shoulders and will not meet his eye. "Yarrow's short," she says. "So it's greedy."

"There is more yarrow in the hills than you pick in a year," says Hippocrates.

Delphia stays silent.

"Usual price, or I pick it myself."

"Tomorrow," says Delphia meekly. "Same cost."

We laugh as the rogue woman limps away. "I can never tell," says Hippocrates, "how much Delphia knows about medicines."

"We should give *something* for this three-day fever," says Nicodemus.

"No treatment. It is wrong to give medicine for the sake of it," says Hippocrates. "Give nothing."

"The patients expect treatment."

"The body must heal itself. Few understand. We must be on our way. Look in on Tellis, please Philo."

"Tellis is ill, too?"

"Will be. Never likes to miss an illness."

Timocrates and I call at the house of Tellis as the sun begins its slow fall. As Hippocrates predicts, Tellis lies on his couch.

"I hear you mean to take the fever," Timocrates begins.

"I have got the fever," says Tellis. "I can feel a serious case coming on."

"Rest and a light diet of gruel," says Timocrates. "You will be fine in two days."

Tellis sneezes. "What sort of doctor are you? Have I fever with the kidney, or fever with the flux?" He sniffs noisily, and energetically fans himself.

I examine his eyes, his breathing and his throat. "No fever, Tellis. You have a common cold."

"Me? A cold?"

"If you do get a fever, it will last three days and then be over. Crisis on the third day. Take it easy then. That is what is happening to everyone," Timocrates explains.

"Too simple, my friend, quite artless," an oil-smooth voice informs us. A man was in the ante-room the whole time and now walks up to the couch. I recognise Euryphon of Cnidus.

The smile is permanent, but the lips are thin. He lingers lovingly over his own words, which glide from him, rich as honey. They match the lushness of his tunic with its silk-woven hem and gold clasp on the shoulder of his cloak.

"My wise and beneficent eyes," says Euryphon smoothly, "perceive the fascinating plights of this municipality. Fever of the intestines with a slimy cough. So grievous. Flushing of the lungs with congealing of the liver. Ah, the foam and the pangs. Overheating in the cranium with pithy bronchials. Three-day fever, indeed. What simple notions. And, you know, Tellis is especially interesting." He smiles at Tellis, relishing the symptoms in their rich variation.

Tellis smirks. "Fever with the irritable nose," he says triumphantly, "combined with watering eyes."

"You have only a cold, Tellis, not even the three-day fever," I repeat.

"Simplify if you must," purrs Euryphon, "but there is such exuberance of dissimilarity in, say, Bion the potter, in Niarchos in the street of the shoemakers, in Philiscus..."

"These are our patients."

"Were. Now they single out my genius."

"Three-day fever, all of them," says Timocrates, "for which there is no treatment."

"You are young to debate with confidence. A mere leveret."

"You will see for yourself if you examine them."

Euryphon taps his forehead. "Medicine belongs up here. I never stare at a patient, scrounging inspiration."

"Hippocrates would disagree."

"Ah, Hippocrates. A naive man." Euryphon shrugs his shoulders, as if all is explained. "A doctor who shrinks to purge. He would not succour you with soothing herbage, Tellis, my friend."

"You are my doctor," says Tellis. He likes treatment. He likes plenty of it. "Luckily, I do not need a purge."

"What will you do for his cold?" asks Timocrates suspiciously.

"Attend and appreciate the enviable art of medicine." Euryphon smiles at Timocrates and me in turn. "First, the system will be scoured of evil biles and gases."

"Well, I..." begins Tellis.

"On whom do you rely?" purrs Euryphon.

"You."

"He would do better to blow his nose," says Timocrates.

Euryphon smiles, as if tolerating a childish joke. "Tellis will be the vessel for an individually prescribed diet of whey."

"Whey gives you stomach ache," I point out. "You will like that, Tellis. Something real to complain about."

Euryphon waves us away contemptuously, and leans over Tellis with a lubricating smile.

Tellis, too, waves us away. We can only leave.

As we walk off from the house, Alexander, the merchant who bought my father's couch, waddles up. "Where is Hippocrates? I cannot find him anywhere. My wife. She is near death." Alexander is chewing figs, taking them one after the other from a pouch.

Timocrates fetches Hippocrates, and we go together to the house of Alexander.

CHAPTER SIX

"Remember I am a rich man, I can pay for the best," says the merchant, stuffing in another fig.

His wife, Elena, lies frail and white-faced, unable to focus her eyes. Her forehead is hot to touch. There are other symptoms too, abdominal pain and swelling of the ankles. Hippocrates feels the heat of her brow and notes the breathing.

"The fever again," he nods. "But with complications."

"She is so hot," says Alexander. "I have tried to bring down the temperature. Delphia sold me feverfew, at twice the price, mind you. And willow tea, too, but it makes no difference." He takes chunks from a loaf he grabbed from a table in passing, and stuffs them into his mouth.

"Another doctor offered to treat her. He suggested a purge, but she is too weak for that. I did not trust his smooth manner."

"Euryphon?"

Alexander nods.

"Sensible," says Hippocrates. "He discovers patients better than he heals." There is a long pause.

"Follow my argument carefully. We know illness produces heat. It *seems* wise to reduce temperature. However, heat is not a symptom of sickness, but that which heals. We should increase the heat of the body, not reduce it."

"She is so hot. We must make her cool," insists Alexander.

"The body needs heat to cure itself." Hippocrates takes the merchant by the shoulders as if to force understanding into his head. "I have observed patient after patient. More patients than you have seen ships. *Heat heals the body.*"

Alexander looks at the sweat on his wife's forehead. "I have never heard that before."

Hippocrates looks at him steadily. "I have observed it." He looks down at the sick woman again. "Elena is critical. To raise the temperature is the one chance."

"I can pay for anything."

"It is not a matter of money."

"Who else can I trust?" Alexander tenderly wipes his wife's brow again. "Yes, all right."

Even Alexander, who prices usually only with coin, recognises the power within Hippocrates, the force for good, with the strength of integrity. Alexander would not be a man to value goodness normally, but he realises its power at this moment.

Hippocrates makes a concoction of yarrow, so strong that he needs to sweeten it with honey. When it is cool enough, Alexander helps his wife to drink, though she is weak as one in the presence of Atropos.

"Is that all you can do?"

Hippocrates nods. "I will be back at noon," he promises.

We expect many calls today from those with the fever, but instead, patients turn to the man with the honey tongue. They are impatient of time's own cure; they welcome his diagnosis that they are unique.

"It is not fair," says Cratis. "It would be different if he were a good doctor. We should prescribe more."

"That would help us. Not the patient," says Hippocrates.

There are still matters about which we are ignorant. But Euryphon does not recognise his own limitations.

Xenia is in the yard. She pours water from a pot onto the pale parched soil of the herb garden. "Delphia said

76

which plants like plenty."

Two weeks ago the leaves began to show, some feathery, some spiky, others grey and hairy. Now the corner dances with aromatic, health-giving life. The plants spill over the border of white pebbles, exuberant and pushing one against the other as they strengthen.

Perhaps it is pride in the garden that makes Xenia stand more elegantly, bending her knees to reach the earth, instead of sticking her behind in the air like a pecking hen.

Mother puts her stool near to the herbs, so that their smell wafts up to her as she embroiders ribbons.

Delphia is in the market place again. "Will you buy?" she croaks to me. She has abandoned the policy of supply and demand; her basket is once more brimming with plants.

"Poppy to operate, and a little for yourself besides?" She smiles up at me, her cracked mouth scarcely able to move.

"No thank you, Delphia. Hippocrates distrusts poppy."

"Mandrake makes you happy," whispers the old woman. "Takes away the sadness of the world. Happy spirits in these old roots of mine."

"Mandrake destroys the mind."

"Hellebore drive off bad spirit. Ergot hurry on the baby, all nice and quickly."

"No thank you, Delphia. But I could do with some dandelion root. It is helpful with dropsy."

"Very nice with dropsy," agrees Delphia. "But poor Delphi has none."

"No dandelion root at all?"

"No."

"Oh, well. Now why is it you cannot treat yourself?" I note her peeling mouth and scaly hands, and remember how she advised Xenia on the herbs.

"I will give you some unguent for your dry skin." I take a jar of olive oil emulsified with egg, from the bag Xenia made. "Put that on your skin. It will be milder than those concoctions of yours."

"Thankie, kind Philo." Delphia shakes her head with pleasure, unused to compassion. "I bring you, dearie, my juicy roots." Carefully, she puts the little pot in her basket. But I imagine she may sell it further up the road, claiming it is nectar from Egypt.

Pausing at the sandal stall to recall my thong-cutting days, I can still see Delphia meandering in the crowd, handling her herbs and muttering over them to attract custom. Euryphon approaches her.

"What life-restoring roots reside in your panniers, old woman?" His hands reach towards the baskets.

Delphia thrusts the baskets to her side. "What you pay old Delphie, then?" she whines.

I pick up, over the sounds of the market, his high offer. Delphia stares up at him, stepping forward to look closely, almost menacingly, into his face. Then she smiles. She forages deep in her basket, and draws out three long roots.

Dandelion, they look like to me. So much for the favours of old Delphia. No doubt she knows who is the most popular doctor in the town.

Elena still lies hot and restless, clutching at her stomach as the pain twists within her.

Hippocrates gives another dose of yarrow.

"Try something else," pleads Alexander.

"There *is* nothing else. The body must fight

78

to recover."

We wait until she falls into a shallow sleep, and leave Alexander crunching barley cake beside his wife's couch.

In a corner of the market Euryphon trades with Delphia. From one basket she pulls out a fistful of leaves, and from the other, roots, the shape of the dangerous black hellebore. She trades for coins and watches Euryphon walk away before she hobbles off, laughing to herself.

Hippocrates goes home to write up all the notes he made in the travels of his earlier years. I decide to start a paper on the treatment in acute disease, but Timocrates says we must go to the stadium. "The Archon is there, and others of the council."

The Chief Archon sits half-way up the track on the small mound so that he can see the whole stadium. His tunic gleams, the finest cotton from Egypt, and his hair is curled carefully across his forehead. Rings on each hand wink in the sun. He is attended by two others, equally pristine, almost as grand.

We are all eager to race, to be seen.

Timocrates and I take our places at the starting sills. There is a thumping in my chest even before the race begins. By contrast, Timocrates looks cooler and more certain of himself than ever. Nicodemus poses alongside us with a confident smile.

From the first length Timocrates leads by his own height. He turns alone at the post. It is not a day to lurk cleverly at the back. Nicodemus and I move shoulder to shoulder. Nicodemus, his head high, glides easily, as if he is not even trying. I strive from the first moment. We turn, hands together on the post.

We are still together on the twenty-third length. Nicodemus does not surge forward and it is certain I will beat him. With my eyes on the figure ahead, I see Timocrates as if we are up in the hills. I remember the morning I beat him, the one time I ever have.

I can do it; I have done it before.

In the last ten strides I find my strength, and Nicodemus seems to slide back out of sight. But Timocrates flies. There is none to match him.

I sink to the ground heaving, but Timocrates prances about as if he is warming up. He cannot resist glancing towards the Archon.

"He must have been impressed," I admit. "You did it so easily. He must nominate you."

"Money counts," says Timocrates. "I can win every race here, but I shall never be certain to compete until I walk under that great arch to the track."

"The honour of Cos depends on the athletes. If you are the best, they must choose you."

"We only see the Astipalea runners. But I hear there is one in Chora who moves like a hound."

"There is also the pentathlon. I have never seen a javelin thrown so far as you throw it." Nicodemus feels magnanimous.

"I am not counting on *anything*."

We meet again at dusk to visit our few remaining patients.

"Four days," says Hippocrates. "The fever will leave the town."

"In that time," says Cratis, anxious as a fledgeling waterfowl on the bank, "we will have lost all our patients to Euryphon. I think we should give some sort

80

of medicine even if it is useless."

"No."

"It makes sense, Hippocrates," says Nicodemus.

"I am not from Cnidus." The hurt expression shows his disappointment in us.

Tellis's slave buys fish in the market.

"How's your master?" I ask as he sniffs over the catch.

The slave chooses red mullet. "He vomits and his head aches. He has a high fever, he says."

"He did not have a fever before Euryphon treated him; he only had a cold."

"The doctor believes Tellis is a most interesting man. He is to have more treatment."

We visit Elena early. Alexander is eating white cheese; he carries a large platter of it in one hand. "She is no better."

"One day more," says Hippocrates. "Fever will rise again today. Certain of this. The yarrow will combine with the healing force of the body."

"She is a lovely woman, and I am fat. I would not find another such wife. I could buy many a wife, but not one to love me as she does." Alexander nods, and sits beside his wife, little crumbs of white cheese falling onto the white cotton sheet.

It is shortly before first light the following morning when the servant of Tellis sends for us. Hippocrates, Cratis and myself all go to see him.

"He is dying. Bent like an acrobat with pain. His eyes wobble."

Tellis seems in a poor way. His moans and shouts have woken most of the street. There are murmurings for the first time against Euryphon.

"Treatment?" Hippocrates asks.

"Black hellebore, the doctor gave."

Convulsions follow if black hellebore is given to the healthy. Tellis also knows this. Observation shows there is no fever, or only in the patient's imagination.

Tellis opens his eyes wider, and starts to roll about, foaming at the mouth.

"Are the convulsions genuine?" asks Cratis.

Tellis becomes more spectacular in his writhing, to prove they are.

"How bad is the pain?"

"What?" Tellis pauses.

"Barley water. And sleep." Hippocrates turns to go. "See to him, Cratis."

Tellis calms down. He will not waste his performance on mere students.

"What is that?" he asks of the cup that Cratis produces.

Cratis winks at me. "Poppy," he whispers to Tellis.

"I thought Hippocrates..."

"Hush, there are times when even he..."

"Ah," says Tellis, gratified. He gulps it down.

After an impressive display of diminishing anguish, Tellis falls asleep. It has been a busy day for him.

"Those were not real convulsions, were they?" Cratis frowns.

"I think not."

"But he has taken black hellebore."

Delphia is huddled up beside a stall for the day is colder.

"How are the sores?" I ask.

"Much better."

"They look exactly the same to me."

She smiles up at me, wily as ever.

"You have not used the ointment, have you Delphia? Did you sell it?"

"Delphi has paid her debt," she croaks.

"By providing Euryphon with medicine for Tellis, I suppose."

"And for the lady of Alexandi. True." She meets my eye, unusually direct.

"What?" says Hippocrates. "A purge of black hellebore will kill her."

But he is wrong. At this moment, Alexander strolls into the market place, a sticky honey cake in his pudgy hand.

"My wife recovers," he says. "The fever has left her and she sleeps."

"As I predicted," says Hippocrates, still staring at Delphia.

"I have a confession, Hippocrates. It is Euryphon I have to thank," says Alexander. "I could bear it no longer, the waiting. I trusted you, but..."

"What did Euryphon give her, Delphia?" I ask.

"Wonderful woman," says Alexander, and throws his arm round her dirty shoulders. "A wonderful cure you provided."

Delphia must limp away quickly unless she wants Hippocrates' wrath on her head. But the old crone sidles closer and starts to cackle.

"That foreign doctor from old Cnidi doesn't know the roots. Those roots no cure. No harm neither. Not even tiny twinges. Doesn't know his hellebore from his turnips. Eh?" She digs her fingers into my arm. "Or a dandelion from a parsnip. Old Delphi help her friends, don't you forget." She hobbles off, muttering to herself.

Cratis nods, pleased. "I knew those convulsions

were odd."

"So Euryphon gave your wife turnips for her fever, Alexander. What say you now?"

Alexander goes pink, like a rosy, overgrown piglet. "You will never forgive me. So little faith in you."

"Understandable. No further mention."

Alexander recovers. "He could have killed my wife. I will have that man off the island."

"He gave Tellis a pain for the first time in his life," says Cratis, "with turnips." He makes a note on the hem of his tunic to remind him to repeat the joke later.

"The whole town will know about this," Alexander promises, and waddles away, chewing another honey cake.

"Old Delphia is no fool," smiles Hippocrates. "My notes must wait." He strolls towards the plane tree. "We must be available again."

# CHAPTER SEVEN

In the late spring, sacred heralds from the mainland sail into harbour, three of them. They proclaim that the games will take place at Olympia, at the time of the second full moon after the summer solstice. My head is dizzy at the glorious sight of them. Even more for what they might mean to us.

Two days later, from the shade of the plane tree, we watch the Archon walk up to the rails beneath the altar of Zeus where the public notices are displayed. He hammers a new papyrus among the other information.

"Timocrates, I ask again," says Hippocrates, "how many days for the collar bone to mend?"

But Timocrates can only stare at the Archon, yearning to know, yet terrified to discover if the athletes are named for Olympia.

Hippocrates smiles. "Is something more important than the collar bone? Well, lecture finished."

Timocrates runs to the notice. I cannot run. I walk slowly, not daring to see what is written there.

Timocrates shrieks, kneels head down on the cobbles and beats his fists triumphantly on the ground.

The first thing that I see is the name of Timocrates heading the athletes, chosen for not only the twenty-four length foot race, but the pentathlon as well.

Scanning the other names, my stomach contracts. The board before me goes momentarily black.

My name is not on the notice. Neither is that

of Nicodemus.

The other place in the foot race is Simonides of Chora, the man Timocrates has spoken of. I have heard of Simonides, a brute of a man, with a temper black as Hades.

Not immediately can I turn to Timocrates, now back on his feet. When I do, my words are quieter than I intend. "It is you for all of us. May luck go with you."

This afternoon, Nicodemus does not run. He sits beside the track, ignoring all that pass. He is still sitting there, staring up into the hills when I come out of the bath house.

"I feel bad, too, Nicodemus. But pleased for Timocrates. He was frightened the council would ignore a poor man."

Nicodemus still stares at the dark cypress trees on the hills. "I am pleased, too," he says mechanically.

"Then stop looking so cross."

"A man might have more than the games on his mind."

"I am sorry." Hesitating to ask what is wrong, I wait, wondering if it would be more tactful to go or stay.

"Why? Why?" asks Nicodemus. "Why should it happen to me?"

"What?"

Nicodemus stares at me. "Everyone will know in time, and they will laugh. They will say they always knew there must be a flaw in Nicodemus."

"What are you talking about?"

Nicodemus pauses. He looks up into my face, as if wondering whether to confess or not. Eventually he says, "It is Menon. My son. He cannot walk."

"Is he old enough?"

CHAPTER SEVEN

"Of course he is old enough. He is almost two. He
should have walked moons ago. He is clever, you know;
he talks quite marvellously. His fingers are nimble. But
one foot...is not as it should be."

"What is wrong?"

"He has...what is called a club foot. The toes are all
bent up."

I can think of nothing to say.

"My child," says Nicodemus, "*my* child...not perfect."

Nicodemus has the right to expect his whole life will
be golden with success; the gods have endowed him
with every possible gift until now.

"Has Hippocrates seen him?"

"My cousin's child," says Nicodemus slowly, "has a
club foot. It was treated with the knife. Not in this
town. Ever after, the whole leg has hung heavy and
lifeless. I could not bear to see Menon like that. I cannot think about it." Nicodemus walks away with shoulders bent under their burden.

However, Nicodemus and his wife Alexis *do* bring
Menon to see Hippocrates later that day, while I am
at his house potting up some ointment. Alexis is a
beautiful woman. To have such a wife is a tribute to
Nicodemus. Her usually serene face echoes her husband's anxiety.

Hippocrates takes Menon on his knee. "Here is the
trouble-maker. This muscle at back of leg pulls too
tight."

"Can it be loosened?" asks Alexis. "Without the
knife?"

"Bandaging. Safer than the knife."

"Do you think he will walk?" asks Nicodemus
tensely.

"Certainly. He will run, I hope."

"He is so little to be all bandaged up," says Nicodemus. He sees Menon as lame for life, unable to wrestle or walk without limping. Unable to excel, for ever to be marked out as lame. For Nicodemus, there is no greater reflected disgrace.

Hippocrates manipulates the limb, stretching the muscle which is pulling the foot down and curling the toes. But he is so gentle that Menon does not cry.

Holding it like this, he bandages the foot over a piece of stiff leather, padded with wool soaked in olive oil. "No cold toes, Menon."

"Those toes cold," says Menon, pointing to the other foot.

"So quick in the mind," says Nicodemus.

"Lydia," calls Hippocrates, "your needle please, and some coarse thread." His elder daughter is often in the courtyard watching her father work.

Lydia gives him her needle, and Hippocrates loops the bandage under the foot, stitching the end to the bandage below the knee. "Tighten bandage daily. Resew. Muscle will stretch. Slowly."

Lydia, as she waits for her needle back, whispers to Alexis, "There is nothing my father cannot do. The leg will be perfect." She smiles at the older woman, totally serene.

I smile at Lydia, with her sand-pale hair and summer-blue eyes. With a shock, I realise how close she is to being a woman.

"Use strengthens," says Hippocrates. "Encourage him to walk."

Menon's leg, bandaged up, is almost as big as the rest of him. As Alexis carries him home, she cannot hide her tears. Nicodemus lets her go and comes with me to the market place, his face still tight with distaste for the clumsy bundle that is Menon's leg.

"Timocrates is chosen for the games," I announce on arriving home. "Two events."

Mother bends over her embroidery. "I am pleased for him. The Archon and council are not always just in their choice."

"He should have gone to the games in Athens," says Agatha. "The winner gets a jar of olive oil there, not a useless wreath of leaves."

"Women should compete in the games. And slaves," says Xenia.

"You should have been a Spartan," I tell her. "The girls in Sparta train with exercise in order to be strong, son-bearing wives. Women with muscles."

"I would have more dignity than to go running back-wards and forwards like a bead on the abacus," says Agatha.

"Sometimes," says Xenia, "before I go to the market, I go up into the hills and run fast, like you used to, Philo. I run just to feel the wind against my face. No-one else is there so early, when there is still mist on the water and the hills look blue like spring anemones. Then I believe anything might come true."

"That is not being womanly," I tell her, "rushing about in the hills like that. You should try to be more...more serene." The word sums up what is best in a woman.

"Being womanly," says Xenia, "is being perceptive." She flounces out of the weaving room, turning to say over her shoulder, "I could run faster than Timocrates if I got the chance. And by the way, Cratis was here looking for you today."

After this, I notice she does not mention running with the wind on her face again. And she walks with smaller, daintier steps.

Xenia is not the only one who wants to be different. I put a lick of olive oil on my couchgrass hair to create order. It does not, and the oil seeps down my neck.

One day, when Hippocrates is checking his foot bandage, Menon sees Timocrates run into the courtyard to collect some medicine; Timocrates never walks where he can run. For some reason, Menon is attracted by the bright green design on the border of his tunic. The child waves after him as he collects the thyme and marjoram he wants.

"Can you spare me a bit of that bandage?" Timocrates asks.

"No," says Menon. "Makes me better."

"When you have really finished with it, I will exchange it for my tunic," says Timocrates as he leaves.

Menon beams round. "Tim...Timotes is my friend."

"Walking yet?" enquires Hippocrates.

"No."

"His mind needs the idea." He has noticed Menon's interest in Timocrates. "Take him to the stadium to watch the athletes."

"To attend to the child is woman's work. And Alexis cannot go to the stadium."

"You can take him."

"There are people there."

Hippocrates looks at Nicodemus gently. "Do not be ashamed. Some gifts are not given. Opportunity must be created."

Nicodemus takes Menon to the stadium. Ignoring his friends, he puts the child down on the ground near a low fence to watch and stands slightly apart.

Cratis decides to throw the discus. He is twirling round in the middle of the field, and drops the weight on his foot. Menon rolls over on his back, laughing.

"Sit up," says Nicodemus through his teeth.

Timocrates throws himself along the track, white sand spraying up under his strong feet, hair flying out behind him. Menon watches, anchored to the earth by his great bandage.

Nicodemus stares round him, embarrassed. Timocrates thunders past, sweat on his forehead, sweat running down his back. Menon watches him all the way to the turning post and all the way back. Then very slowly, clumsy as a bear, he pulls himself to his feet by hauling on the fence. He lets go to wave to Timocrates at the end of the track. He hovers, he wobbles, he totters over. But for one brief moment, Menon stands alone.

Timocrates comes over to him after bathing. "Young man," he says. "You did better than I. You achieved something today which you have never done before. But I did not. We must strive harder."

Menon nods, suddenly shy that such a man should be speaking to him.

Nicodemus does not bring him regularly to the track, although Menon often asks to come. Nicodemus prefers to push him on the swing he has made and hung from the tree in the yard. Sitting on it, Menon swings freely through the air, squeaking with pleasure like any other child.

Only when Menon begs and Alexis pleads will Nicodemus carry him to the stadium in the afternoon, the bandaged leg stuck out behind them. As soon as

they arrive at the track, Menon looks round for Timocrates who is not always there. He might be wrestling
or jumping with weights in his hands.

But today in the field Timocrates has set himself a
mark he must reach with the javelin before he sails for
the games.

"I have a second dream now," he confides in me as
he prepares his grip on the spear.

"To win two crowns?"

"That, too. You know, I have thought for some time
that my father must have been an athlete. I believe he
will be watching the games."

"You torment yourself."

"Would this impress a father?"

He makes his run. He hoists the weapon. He strikes
the mark. Shouting, he rushes up the field to check.
Menon, already standing up to watch, lurches forward,
and without holding on to anything, takes his first step,
slowly heaving his great bundle of bandage over the
grass.

"He walks, Nicodemus."

"Yes. I suppose you could say that."

I lie on the grass above the town. The disappointment
poisons me; it is a physical pain. The glory of which
Timocrates and I dreamed all through our school days
has been wrenched from me. Worse, I cannot blame
the council because they did not overlook Timocrates;
they did not favour only the rich men's sons.

I go over in my mind how it might have been. I go
over that a hundred times. I am tired, as if I have been
in the race.

I have come here many days to the balm of the hills,
and now, at last, I come to terms with my pain. And

my jealousy.

I am ready to go home. The disappointment is wrapped up inside me, never to be shown to anyone. It will shrivel away.

Instead, I will be proud for my friend and rejoice with him. For Timocrates is truly Apollo's child. As he runs in that most famous of all stadiums, he will glow with a light that is gold.

When I get back to the house, Xenia looks closely at me.

"I am glad that is over, Philo. You have been looking mean."

This morning I treat a foul-smelling gangrenous wound, and all I want now is some fresh, cool air. I walk down to the shore to breathe the clean, salt smell, not where the harbour holds the stink of fish, but where the sand is soft and white, and flecked with foam; where there is nothing between man and the island of Nissiros which Poseidon flung into the sea in his rage.

I breathe in the sparkling air and feel cleansed. Walking on the shore is such a strange thing to do that I am surprised to find others there.

Nicodemus is sitting on the sand with Menon on his knee. They are busy with some sort of game. I do not want to pry, but watch for a moment before turning away.

Nicodemus arranges a row of pebbles at the edge of the sea, where white foam skates up the beach before turning and shushing back.

"Can Menon kick the pebble into the water before it runs away?" asks Nicodemus gently. He holds the boy's leg, small now, without its bandages, so that the foot must do all the work, flicking sideways against the pull of the short, tight muscles.

"I cannot."

"Let us try again."

The foam curd draws near, Menon wriggles and strikes out with his leg.

"Very nearly," says Nicodemus. "Menon, we will do it this time, you and I. Think only of your best."

"How Timocrates will do it?"

"Yes."

While I watch, Menon at last manages to kick the pebble with the weak muscles. Nicodemus claps his hands.

I creep away, the sand muffling my steps.

And when I arrive home, I find the Archon standing beside our gate.

# CHAPTER EIGHT

The Archon sees me as second best, but he has no choice.

Simonides of Chora, chosen for the foot race, was always a brute. Yesterday, he killed a slave in a fight over three goats. Those guilty of a blood crime cannot compete at Olympia.

"It has been carefully considered in the council," the Archon says, with such disdain that his top lip looks likely to disappear up his nose. "We conclude that you must go in his place. And since you are a...er ...poor man, certain money of Simonides has been confiscated for his crime, and will pay for your passage there."

He looks me up and down. "I trust you are grateful for your good fortune. Simonides was, after all, an aristocrat, and would have brought glory upon the island through his success." He sighs deeply. "We have to send you in his place."

"I will not let you down. I am deeply grateful to the council and to yourself." The world is full of singing birds and, like hope, they fly higher and higher.

When I tell them at home, my mother and Xenia both cry.

"My child," says Mother. "My child, running with men as grand as the statues."

Xenia muffles her feelings in preparations for the

evening meal.

"You are pleased for me?" I ask.

"Of course I am, Philo."

"Tears of joy then," I laugh, and touch her shoulder with sudden brotherly warmth.

She looks up. "Now you seem so far away."

The vines are blue with fruit, their stems tiered with mist-veiled grapes. The time of the first full moon after the grape harvest arrives. Timocrates and I leave in the boat, along with the other athletes from all over the island, to test our skills at the greatest of all the games. Timocrates looks the fittest of any, and carries more sensible hopes with him. If he wins, we will all walk taller.

"The luck of the gods be with you," says Nicodemus, who has come to see us off.

Timocrates shrugs. "The gods might be with us every one. In the end it will be the man himself who wins or loses."

The boat sails westward round the island. I had hoped we might go to Piraeus, port of Athens. But we are to sail to the west coast of the Peloponnese, for that is the cheapest route. Long after the faces on the shore are indistinct, I can see where Nicodemus still watches.

I feel sorrow for him, and a fear of my own failing.

We arrive at Olympia only just in time to take the oaths, for there are two storms at sea. They do not make an interesting story, as I spend most of the time being sick.

We swear we are free of blood guilt, will train properly, and will not cheat in the competitions.

The training in the daytime is hard, we work for longer than at home in the stadium. Here there are professional trainers, so called, but they are rough men, pushy, and they teach me nothing I do not know already.

Yesterday, we sacrificed at the great altar of Zeus, and there were youths' races in the afternoon. But today, the second day, is the real beginning of the competition with the horse races this morning. Timocrates and I find ourselves room to stand at the back of the embankment which surrounds the hippodrome, to watch the four-horse chariot races.

Timocrates is ambivalent. One side of him is envious that any man can be wealthy enough to own four splendid horses and, being envious, he turns against the man and despises him for having a soft, aristocratic life; for not being like us, appearing at the games against the odds.

But another side of him is full of genuine admiration for the charioteer in his long white tunic, controlling four animals whose individual strengths far outweigh that of their master. "It is the power of the mind," says Timocrates, and his hands are turned around imaginary reins.

There have been heats, and we await the final between four chariots.

"And three owned by one man," a voice behind informs us. "He entered seven chariots in all. No-one can recall the like."

"*One* man?" says Timocrates, with disbelief.

"Alcibiades," our informant nods. "The soldier. Wearing the red headband."

Alcibiades is tall and handsome, with a full sneering mouth. His eyes, we can see from here, are large and brown, yet they lack warmth. In contrast, there are those lines around his eyes and mouth which suggest he laughs a great deal.

Alcibiades starts so quickly, it is as if the trumpet blows to his will. He stands braced against the floor of the chariot, head thrown back, and lashing the air with a long whip. At the same time he shouts, "Faster, you fools. Drive harder," to the other chariots, two of which he owns. His lips are drawn back over his teeth like those of a remorseless wolf.

"What a man," says Timocrates, never taking his eyes off the buffeting tunic.

"Do you think he would be pleased if one of his other chariots won?" I speculate.

"No-one could beat that man. He is invincible."

It is no surprise that Alcibiades takes the honour of first, and his other chariots second and fourth.

As he drives out of the hippodrome, gifts are handed to him, the councillors bow. The crowd press forward to touch him. He drives carelessly forwards, ignoring them all.

Timocrates says nothing, but he smoulders with the conviction that he could be equally contemptuous, given high birth.

It is good that we see Alcibiades; it sets Timocrates up for the pentathlon this afternoon. I watch some of this at the beginning, but train, too, not to be idle the day before my own chance of glory.

His less good disciplines are first, discus and long jump, and he is fourth and third in these. But now he prepares himself for the javelin.

He balances it at shoulder height, relishes the poise of it, tests the ratio of its weight with his own. Now he runs. Faster. Faster. Leans back. Gathers himself. Compresses his energy.

He lofts the spear.

It chases up into the sky, soaring, soaring, graceful as a swift on the wing.

It is as if the javelin, too, holds its breath, prolonging its freedom.

Until it glances down, oblique to the last moment, to land far, far beyond the mark of those gone before. The spectators love him for that throw.

A close victory in the sprint puts Timocrates in the lead for the pentathlon crown, with only the wrestling to go.


We mingle with the crowds in the palaestra, and become aware of a strange coincidence. Favourite for the wrestling and lying second, is another Timocrates.

It is not an uncommon name, but Timocrates stares at his namesake, unable to drag his eyes away. He whispers to me, "Is he not like me?"

"I know what you are thinking. It is just your imagination."

"Do as I ask. Find out from which state he comes."

I walk away, and enquire casually of a spectator, "Is that tall fair man by the water trough, Timocrates from Samos?"

"No. He is Timocrates from Athens. Son of one of the nine Archons of the city state of Athens."

I walk away, overawed.

"He is from Athens," I pass on the information.

"I guessed it would be so." Timocrates is as white as a lily.


Standing slightly apart, I watch a small play acted out.

Timocrates of Athens is beside a man in a fine white robe who, I suppose, might be his father. This man moves away and speaks privately to one in a blue cloak, at the same time pointing to my Timocrates, who is watching the wrestling, his eyes not focussed on it.

Now the man in the blue cloak comes over and speaks to Timocrates. "I am told, young man, you are weak in the wrestling event. But you put up a rousing display with the javelin. You should not go un-rewarded. Would you accept some compensation for disappointment in the last element?"

Timocrates examines him carefully, thinking as he looks. "You try to bribe me," he observes. "Why?"

"There are others with all-round excellence. Your talent with the javelin..." he searches for a convincing story.

Timocrates looks over to his namesake, and notices, as I have, that he stands beside the older man.

He nods slowly. "Do you come from *his* father?"

The man in the blue cloak sucks in his lips, wondering what would be the cleverest approach.

Timocrates smiles broadly, showing his teeth, "Tell that man his son will win the pentathlon." His eyes are wide, and not a little wild.

"You have taken a bribe," I say, when the blue cloak is lost in the crowd.

"Do you not see?" Timocrates grabs me by my shoulders. "You *must* have realised. I have found my father. And my half-brother, too."

"You cannot know that. Yes, he does resemble you, but that is not proof."

"I felt from the moment I saw him that I knew him.

I have accepted no money. And when I win, I shall reveal myself."

Timocrates thinks only that he has found his father. And that he will impress him.

"Timocrates..."

"What?"

"Nothing."

"Find out more," he implores. Reluctantly, I mingle with the crowd.

I arrive beside the older man when the one in the blue cloak is nowhere about. I cannot think he will recognise me as a friend of Timocrates, I am not distinguished.

"Timocrates should do well here," I say, as if to a neighbour.

"Athens is proud of her sons," smiles the older man, pleased at what appears to be my interest.

I apologise. "I was thinking of Timocrates of Cos," I tell him with extreme courtesy, "though the Athenian is a fine athlete also."

"My son, yes," muses the man. "He is a fine athlete."

Well, that is one fact established. He is the father of at least one Timocrates.

He looks at me and asks casually, "You support him because you, too, are from Cos?" He is so casual that he has to concentrate. He makes a show of staring out across the crowd.

"Oh yes. We run together in the foot race tomorrow."

"Tell me...is he also the son of an athlete? I mean, his father...is he the sort of man who did well on the track?" Again he pretends not to be interested in an answer. I pause, and say nothing.

He turns now, to look at me with a great deal of care. This man is not making small talk.

And I know for certain that Timocrates is right.

"I do not know his father." I hurry back with the good news that it may bear him up in the wrestling.

Timocrates has realised the truth. Clear and stark. He has completely changed.

"My father is a man who offers bribes."

"It was the man in a blue cloak. Not your father, exactly."

"Of course, it came from him."

"And he is your father." I tell him why I am so sure.

"And now I wish he is not," says Timocrates quietly.

His time has come to compete.

I do not think it is disgust. I know it is not the bribe. But Timocrates cannot find his power in the fighting. I think it may simply be shock.

He is thrown three times, and now the crown of olives for this greatest of all competitions is lost to him.

The man in a blue cloak meets us as we emerge from the bath house, "An admirer sends you a little compensation," he whispers.

Timocrates takes the money bag and swings it round his head. He tries to clout the other, but I pull his arm down.

I hand the money bag back. "We are not in the way of bribes," I say, and lead Timocrates, stumbling, away.

It is the night of the full moon, coming as always on the night before the third day which is the time of religious sacrifice.

I know somehow I have to revive Timocrates so that

he may recover his spirit. He is crushed, by defeat, and by the discovery of his father. He is full of self-disgust.

I suggest we go to look at the great statue in the temple of Zeus. It is so impressive there is even a gallery built within the temple for people to see its full beauty from closer to than merely gazing up from the floor. It is more beautiful, even, than the statue of Apollo on the west pediment of the temple; gold and marble, by the hand of Phidias.

But the wonder and beauty of the statue, mysterious in the artificial light of many lamps, fails to move Timocrates. He turns away, and we return to our dormitory without speaking.

On the great funeral mound of the hero Pelops there roast one hundred oxen, sacrifice to great Zeus. In our silent, awed ranks, we process to the altar of Zeus beside the mound, and we make our own sacrifice of the talents of our bodies to the greatest god of all. For it is to honour him that we run.

As we approach, we glimpse, leaving, Timocrates of Athens and his father.

Timocrates follows them with his eyes.

When the heat is past its height come the foot races.

Timocrates had one chance of the crown of olives and failed. He must take his second. But this is my *only* chance. I must stop worrying for him.

We prepare in the athletes' room, oiling our bodies to gleam impressively in the sun. Timocrates of Athens is not here. I do not know if he is in the race.

We walk past the temple of Zeus to go through the corridor into the stadium when the Athenian's father searches us out.

I pull Timocrates away. Another bribe will finish him.

But the man is insistent.

"I have come to apologise," he says. "I had not realised there might be a blood bond."

"Go away," I tell him. "There has been enough damage already."

The man follows us still.

Knowing Timocrates bears his father's name, I say to the older man with all the authority I can assert, "Timocrates of Athens, leave us. Or I shall report the bribe to the authorities."

The man shakes his head.

"I am not Timocrates," he says. "My brother bears that name."

Timocrates spins round, and his face seems bathed in the light from Apollo himself.

"You are not Timocrates?" he shouts. "Then you are not my father?"

"Your uncle, perhaps."

The Athenian is taken aback when Timocrates hugs him and slaps him on the shoulder.

There are tears on Timocrates' face, and a lump like an apple in my own throat.

"You are not my father. My father is not a man who offers bribes."

"I hope that will be forgotten."

"I can forget that now. It is of no importance. Is Timocrates...is my father here?"

"Unfortunately, he is not."

"But you will tell him you have seen his son run at Olympia?"

"I promise you that."

"My father will know," Timocrates tells me as we

run under the arch, "that his son took the crown in the foot race."

The starting sills are warm and rough to the feet. My palms are wet.

I remember the day in the hills when I beat Timocrates.

He is beside me now.

The trumpet blasts, harsh and cold. We are off.

I lead the field. But the feet thunder behind me. If you are small it is better not to see the taller man.

I had meant to start slow, to save myself, but this is not my nature.

Already the crowd shout for their favourites. I hear the name of Timocrates among many.

Timocrates moves up beside me.

He is no longer my friend, nor I his. We are enemies, as we were in the hills, each for ourself.

We turn level at the first five posts.

No-one closes the gap behind us, and half-way through the race I know the crown is between the two of us alone.

Timocrates moves faster. I can still match him.

We turn shoulder to shoulder at the last post.

I grit my teeth. I can do it. I did it in the hills once. Despite the pain in my chest, I edge ahead. The crowd are on their feet. They roar for Timocrates because of the way he throws a javelin; and they roar for me because I might win.

Eight lengths of a man to the line.

Five lengths.

Timocrates has not broken past.

Four.

The crown of olives is within my grasp. It is as the

first time in the hills.

The judges lean forward from their box. The noise fills my ears with a great joy.

Then I hear his rasping breath alongside. I reach for a mirage. And the mirage slips away.

Timocrates pounds ahead. Apollo's child.

He wins. As he always knew he would.

The boat approaches the harbour. As we skirt the shore I can see Nicodemus and Menon with their pebbles among the curds of the trickling waves.

I see Menon pointing to the foaming bow of our caique, the sail puffed out like a corn-fed pigeon's breast. Nicodemus gathers him up, making for the stadium where we will go. They are lost as we round the point.

As Timocrates leads us onto the grass, a shout goes up. He holds up his crown of wild olive, withered now, for them all to see and hurtles down the length of the track.

"Timocrates," shouts Menon, "I can...kick the... pebble, Timocrates." But his voice is lost in the uproar.

Furious at not being heard, Menon lets go of his father's hand, and tugs at his bandage. He pulls it off completely.

Then he sets off up the track after his friend Timocrates. He does not walk. He runs. He runs barefoot up the track, limping, lurching and shouting, but he runs. He has one thought only in his head.

He comes back panting, still not having caught Timocrates. "I am going to run at Olympia, too," he says furiously. "I will make this silly leg run as good as the other. I will."

Nicodemus picks him up, and carries him round the

field for all to see, pounding after the triumphant athletes, both of them as proud as he who knows the glory of the olive crown.

Nicodemus has found this unlikely, this sweet and generous glory. His chilling winter of many months has, at last, dissolved into spring.

# CHAPTER NINE

Has that ephemeral glory changed Timocrates? He sits alone these days or walks by himself in the hills. Often he is down by the harbour, watching the boats come in. Especially, it seems, those from Piraeus, the port of Athens.

"Perhaps it will come soon," I tell him.

"What?"

"The letter from your father. That *is* why you are here?"

"I suppose so." He pauses. "Other problems besides. Do you ever wonder if medicine is any use at all?"

"We have to admit some failures."

"Think of Eulalia. You know her. Severe arthritis. What am I doing? Pretending I can help her. She has not had one day free of pain in seven years."

"Does nothing help?"

"Willow. But the infusion is bitter and makes her sick. There is a blander variety imported from the north. Hippocrates is negotiating with a trading boat to find him some. She is so brave, you know. If she complained more, I would feel less guilty."

"It is not your fault there is no cure."

"Guilty because I am so fit, Philo."

Returning from my patients, I find Mother crying at her loom, distraught, quite unlike in her grief for Father. At first, she is reluctant to explain, but eventually she tells me.

"It is Nichos. My cousin, Nichos. He came to see me. He says I must marry again for the house is without a protector."

"I am the head of our house."

"I told him that, Philo. But he pointed out he is head of the family from which I come. Nichos says you are a youth without your own household."

"Is that how you look on it?"

"Of course not. I am happy with the arrangement. And one day I shall defer to your wife."

"Well, then?"

"He explained you will not marry for years. He was thirty before he took a wife, as most men are. I told him I loved my husband and could not know another man."

"Was that not enough?"

"His wife's brother is recently bereaved and needs a woman to run the household. He sees a happy union within the family. I told him he was after the dowry of the house."

"There is no man to match my father."

"He says you do not support me. That I am forced to earn for you which is degrading. I sent him away at that, but he calls up the street that he will come back to discuss it again."

"I will not let him force you to marry."

"There is nothing you can do. It is the law. Philo, I would not have told you but...and anyway, he is quite wrong. I am not degraded. We are proud of your work."

"Some women," says Agatha "are smiled upon by fate. Two husbands for you, and never a one spare for me."

"There is only one solution." We sit in the yard as I write notes and Xenia strives to restrain the herb garden. It has taken over the yard with purple thyme and aromatic spearmint rampaging across the stones. "I must find a wife. That will make me head of the household, and Mother will be safe."

"You are too young to marry."

"I owe my mother everything. She sacrifices her pride for me to be a doctor. And she works far too hard."

"You must marry for love, Philo, not to save your mother."

"Love is not how you choose a wife, as well you know. A man marries that a wife may run his home well, and bring him honour. Love is incidental." But I think of the way my father loved my mother and envy him.

"You need to marry for love," insists Xenia.

"How would I recognise love?"

"As two lighted windows exactly opposite one another."

"What do you mean?"

"Find out for yourself."

I could not bear to dislike my wife after living in a house where women are loved. Even Agatha is cared for and respected beyond her deserts. Xenia is valued above her station. It is not so in most houses.

I shall need the gods on my side. Demeter is the obvious choice. I go to the temple and sacrifice a small cockerel at the altar. Watching the smoke rise, I pray that I will find more than a wife to run my house and be a mother to my children; I pray that I will find a home for my spirit as well.

Having put Demeter in the picture, I do the same for

Nichos. My mother's cousin lives in a grand house, with a portico on three sides of the courtyard. Within the dining room, preparations for a dinner party are under way. The men's couches are ranged round the walls, and the smell of cooking chicken escapes from the kitchen.

Nichos lounges in a carved chair beside a well. He looks at me scornfully.

I come straight to the point. "I plan to marry soon. My mother will become the dowager in a family arrangement."

"Will she still make goods to sell on the market?" He smirks sarcastically.

"By the spring I shall be able to ask my own fee. So that will not be necessary."

"A healer," says Nichos. "Half a philosopher. Would you tie your mother to that, when she could live in a house such as this. Indeed, my brother-in-law's house has even more rooms."

"It is very fine," I admit. "But she does not want to marry again."

"And who is to be your bride?"

"That is yet to be decided."

Nichos laughs, a loud, humourless laugh. "There is no problem for me, I see." He stands up, and by inclining the palms of his hands towards the gate, indicates it is time for me to go. His guests will soon arrive.

As I leave, the first of them comes in, a fat man decked in a party wreath. He is already drunk.

We sit with Hippocrates in his courtyard, discussing the dangers of trephine brain surgery. It is a hot autumn day. Lydia comes out with a small tray of beakers of honey water to cool us. Over the several moons since I saw her last, she has become fully a woman, with hair braided back so smoothly that her whole head seems moulded in fine alabaster; alabaster, cool as marble to the eye, warm as summer wine to touch.

Something glances against my foot. It is a grass head, a weed growing in the paving. Picking it and crumbling it between my fingers, I realise it is exactly like a head of barley; I hold a sign from the corn goddess, Demeter. She could not have been more explicit.

As I watch, Lydia watches her father for approval and smiles at him. Demeter need not have given such an obvious nudge. Who could be more fitting for a wife than the daughter of my great teacher? And such a beautiful woman would prove me an enviable man.

The matter seems in no doubt until later when I begin to wonder how Hippocrates will view it. I am taller than a year ago. I look in my mother's mirror of beaten bronze. Demeter composed my face with exceptional freedom. When it came to the hair, she was positively negligent.

"Would you ever call me...handsome?" I ask Xenia carelessly as she carries bread to the store-room.

"No." She waves one of the golden-topped loaves under my nose. "Agatha could not bake better than this."

"I am quite tall."

"Mmmm." She shifts more bread. There seems to be a glut; loaves spill out of the store-room.

"The colour of my eyes, see? Like river mud. Unfathomable."

"Cratis has blue eyes."

"Which go watery when the grass heads are full grown."

"But they are very bright in the autumn."

"How do you know about his eyes?"

"He came here today."

"Again?"

"Looking for you."

Cratis is a dull topic. "What about my chin? A strong chin, I would say."

"Magnificent chin."

"You are not being loyal to me, Xenia."

"It is not your face which describes you best." She tugs out some spearmint which is invading the cobbles, bubbling with her own concerns.

"One more year," she says, "and I will have enough money to buy my freedom. Your mother has, at last, named the price."

"You cannot leave us. You have always been here."

Xenia flounces to the door of the weaving room, and leans on the frame. "She will buy a young girl in my place and she asks only the price of such a replacement."

She sticks out her chin, anxious I should not think her price cheap. "Your mother says I am worth more, much more; she would sell me to another only for a vast sum."

"At least the money will help her."

"Is that all you have to say about it?"

"Why does freedom mean so much to you, Xenia? There is little difference between your life, and that of a free woman. It is not as if you were a man, and might want to sit in the council."

"As a slave, I cannot marry a free man," says Xenia, and this time she does not look at me; she scrapes a pattern in the dust with her bare toe.

"Without a dowry?" I laugh at the thought.

She goes back into the weaving room without another word, her hair wild as tamarisk in the breeze.

Since I have no father to arrange a marriage, I must speak for myself. I do not trust Mother. She will become angry if Hippocrates does not immediately appreciate what a fine husband is on offer. Besides, I do not want to tell her my plan until it is positively arranged; she might try to stop me. Be with me now, Demeter.

Hippocrates is not surprised; there is little he does not observe for himself.

"You are very young, Philo. I want Lydia to be happy."

"I can understand if you draw attention to my family poverty, Hippocrates, but I know I could make her happy."

"I love my golden child. Why lose her company?"

I can hardly explain that I want to get married soon to save my mother from unhappiness. Is Demeter with me, or not? I think of Xenia. She does not invoke a god to free her from slavery. She takes it all upon herself. I start again.

"You would like Lydia to marry a doctor?"

He nods.

"And she would be happier with a good doctor?"

"*I* would be."

"Set me a task to prove myself. If I prove a good doctor, will you think again?"

"I like you, Philo. May think again. But not yet."

It is five days later that the news comes from the quarry. A rock fall has struck three men, though none are dead. One is Tellis. I go ahead to his house, where he is carried.

"What was Tellis doing at the quarry?"

"Scrounging for a loan from his brother who works there."

Tellis sweats and is in great pain. Both legs are broken below the knee and the wounds, ground out by the rock, are severe. It is unfair that the injury should be so savage when Tellis could have suffered just as much with half the damage.

An infusion of feverfew reduces his temperature, and a poultice of willow bark eases inflammation until Hippocrates arrives.

"Apollo," cries Tellis. "I call on Apollo. Only the god can heal me now." He sobs piteously.

"In Apollo's absence, we will do our best," I say.

Tellis moves slightly and holds his breath, anticipating the piercing torture in his legs.

"Henbane, Tellis. Exceptional case." Hippocrates waves the leaves in front of him. "Real test."

"A test?" I look at him triumphantly.

Hippocrates bites his lip. He forgets the earlier discussion.

"I..."

"I shall not be found wanting, Hippocrates."

He sighs. "Be spring before these legs mend, Tellis."

Tellis screams, loud and unmusical. Tellis screams louder when he sees Nicodemus and Cratis carry in the fracture bed. The swelling is reduced, and I can set the bones.

"Take this draught. Wine with juice of mandrake. Good strong stuff to stop the pain," I explain. "We must dress the wounds first, Tellis, so that they can heal under the bandages."

"I do not want my legs covered up," says Tellis. "I want to watch them heal." Mandrake works instantly. He speaks quite calmly for Tellis and resigns himself to the dressing.

"Nicodemus, will you support his back?"

"Pull when I say. Get hold of the foot, Cratis, and put a pillow under the knee. I will line the bones up. Right. Now."

"Steady. Steady," says Nicodemus, and wipes Tellis's brow. There is a new compassion about the way Nicodemus deals gently with Tellis.

"Hold it. The bones are in a perfect line." Putting a compress over the fracture line, I begin to bandage, winding the wool tightly at first, to fix the bones, and control the swelling.

"Perfect," says Cratis, and pats Tellis on the foot.

The second leg is quite easy to set.

Tellis lifts his head, and looks down at his legs. "Splints."

"Splints do no good. It is the bandaging that matters."

"I want splints. I have got two broken legs. People might think there are only cuts and bruises."

To keep the patient happy, I make two wooden splints and line them with wool.

Nicodemus goes to visit another patient.

"This will take some time yet. I wish I had food with me, Cratis."

"I will tell your mother as I pass your house."

Very thoughtful of him.

Agatha appears with food. "You are in a mess, Tellis. You will get worse before you are better, no doubt."

"Tellis is fine. Thank you for the food, Agatha." I

unwrap the cloth, to find Agatha has gnawed a ragged wedge out of the bread on her way here.

"Remember my cousin, Philo? Broke her legs. Never walked again. It was a merciful release when she went to Hades."

Tellis, soothed with medicated wine, relishes his injuries.

Eulalia lies on her couch, face hollowed out with pain, hair sparse through her illness. She smiles, her cheeks pulling back from her mouth like the folds of a fan.

"My golden friend," she rasps, and puts out a twisted claw to take Timocrates' sun-tanned hand.

"How is the pain today?"

"Much better." She tries to shift her position, but cannot manage it. We help her to settle more comfortably, but gentle though we are, she cries out twice.

Her daughter brings a bowl of soup.

"I will feed you, Eulalia," says Timocrates.

"I am not keeping you?"

"Who is more important than my favourite patient?" he asks, and lifts the spoon to her mouth as gently as if he is tending the wing of a moth.

To lift her head sufficiently to drink is a struggle, and the meal takes a long time. Eulalia lies back, and smiles gratefully at Timocrates.

"How do you find the new willow bark?" he asks.

"It is lovely. Not a bit sour to drink."

"But does it help the pain?"

"Oh yes. I think so."

"It is for me to help you," he says gently, "not for the patient to be kind to the doctor."

As we leave, Eulalia's daughter says at the gate, "My mother is always happier for your coming."

Further down the street Timocrates shakes his head. "Medicine is a joke."

"Why do it then?"

"At the moment, I see no alternative."

"You have used Hippocrates to further your training for Olympia."

"Yes."

"Have you no satisfaction in helping people?"

"I do not help anyone."

"You help Eulalia."

"Because I speak kindly to her. Because I give her time. Not because I cure the pain."

"You heal her spirit."

"The spirit? I am a man of action, Philo. I have energy. I need to achieve. I cannot find *myself*."

Only now do I realise how depressed Timocrates is. Even so, I am surprised to see tears on his face. Thank the gods there is no-one else to witness them.

"A man takes honour from his father, Philo. I am the son of the brother of an Archon. And yet I am nothing. Less. Half a philosopher."

"How can you win a crown at Olympia, and say you are nothing?"

"The crown has not been acknowledged."

Timocrates is right, of course. He might well expect to wax in a father's pride. Yet he cannot presume even approval.

If only a letter would come from Athens.

# CHAPTER TEN

Winter passes quickly this year and by the early spring, Tellis is close to recovery.

I grind some hyssop leaves in the flour mill, rolling the stone backwards and forwards in the square trough.

Although Xenia should be pleased I am using her herbs, she says, "Wipe the mill out afterwards." She is practising her flute in the sensuous ionic key, which is the most popular at drinking parties. I wish she would not play at these gatherings where the men get drunk and noisy. I remember the guest of Nichos.

"So it is for me, not the slave, to clean the mill?"

"Perhaps it is for me to do today," says Xenia, "but soon now, I will be free. I am the best among the flute girls; my music is requested all the time. I have saved up more drachmas than you have ever seen all together."

"I hope you keep them safe."

"They are in the bank. I have their token."

"Did you put money in a bank?" I ask, taken aback.

She tosses her head and smiles at my surprise. "Cratis did."

"Cratis?"

"Yes. Is he not kind?"

"How did Cratis know about your money?"

"I told him when he came here."

"Has he been here *again*?" Whatever did he want

this time, I wonder.

"He always comes when you are out."

"Typical Cratis."

I leave the flour mill flecked with pale green. "I must visit Tellis now."

"Why do you take so much trouble with one patient?"

"It is my test."

"So that you can be declared a doctor?"

"Not exactly."

"What test then?"

I hesitate. Well, why not confide in Xenia? I have done all my life. "If you really want to know, it is to gain a wife. So that Mother will not be forced to marry again."

"A wife?" says Xenia disbelievingly. "Who?"

"Will you promise not to tell Mother why I want to marry?"

"*Who?*"

"Lydia. Hippocrates' daughter."

"Lydia?"

"Yes."

Xenia stares at me. She says nothing more and goes into the weaving room. But I cannot hear her flinging the shuttle across the loom in her usual noisy way.

When I return home, Xenia is nowhere to be seen, but she has told Mother about me taking a wife, though, as she promised, not the reason why.

"Philo, is Lydia the woman for you?"

"Why should she not be?"

"She is so...frail."

"Lydia is more beautful than any woman I have ever seen. Who else could there be?"

There is a silence.

"I do not know," says Mother, at last.

Timocrates is in the market place, striding between the stalls with restless energy.

"What has happened? Have you had a letter from Athens?"

"No. But I have other news. Marvellous news. A great fleet is being built at Athens. It will sail to conquer Sicily this summer. And who is leading the expedition? Alcibiades, no less."

"Alcibiades in battle. What a sight that would be."

"I shall never forget that glory, Philo. For him, glory is not a fleeting moment at the Olympic games. All his days he lives like a hero from the tales of Homer. There never was such a man on the earth before. All the crowns of Olympia will be nothing beside the glory of fighting under his command."

"What are you talking about?"

"I plan to join the Athenians."

"When?"

"Some time soon."

"You are addicted to glory. It makes you a fool."

"More soldiers are needed than there are men in Athens. They welcome men from the islands, men who can fight on foot. Especially men who can throw a javelin. There will be few cavalry you see, because horses on ships cause chaos."

"You will turn from curing men to killing them?"

"I am a poor doctor. What can I do for Eulalia? But I throw the javelin better than any man in Greece. A man should do that at which he excels. Besides..." Timocrates bites his lip.

"You join the Athenian army in Athens? You think

you will find your father."

"Of course not."

Timocrates leans against the wall of the harbour, watching a boat creep in across the unreal paleness of the early morning sea. He speaks without looking up as I go over to him.

"Eulalia died this morning. She died, crying out in pain." He looks at his hands, spreading out his long fingers, flexing them gracefully. "In five years, her fingers have not stretched out to take food to her own mouth."

"Hippocrates says our skills will take time to perfect. But one day doctors will be able to heal all sickness."

"Maybe. Maybe not. I am leaving for Athens today. I will sail with the war fleet this summer. Javelin throwers are needed to fight from the ships in the sea battles."

"How can you kill men after you have learned to heal?"

"I go for a high ideal, Philo. To own Sicily will restore Athens to her greatness at the time of Pericles. When Athens is great, we, who are her empire, are great."

Hippocrates appears behind us. "No glory. Only blood."

"When Athens is powerful," says Timocrates, "there is peace."

"So men always claim. An excuse."

Timocrates opens his mouth, then thinks better of arguing with Hippocrates. "Will you release me from my contract?"

"No," says Hippocrates. "I will declare you a doctor."

But the flicker of change he hopes to see in Timocrates' eyes is not there.

"I leave today."

We see Timocrates off on the boat, the very same that took us to the games a lifetime ago, and which now takes him to war. He waves bravely, the right shoulder more muscular than the left, but otherwise a perfect figure against the light.

"We need you here, Timocrates," I say in a final attempt to stop him.

"It is the will of the gods," says Timocrates. "I made a sacrifice; I saw it written in the smoke."

"That you must go to war? You saw that in the smoke?"

"No. That I will die, Philo. I saw it plain. Men are speaking well of me, but it is not because I wear a crown of olives. It is because I am a hero."

When Timocrates went to the games, he spurned the luck of the gods; he trusted only in himself. And now he listens to the gods, and they mislead him out of revenge. The gods punish hubris.

The boat slides into the water, the wood creaks as the oarsmen take the craft out to catch the wind.

"Come back," I shout. "You have mistaken the signs, Timocrates. It is easily done."

Timocrates can only wave; all our words now are lost on the voice of the sea.

The pink flowers of the wild almond begin to show in the fields, for it is well into the spring when the time of reckoning arrives. I am worried. When Tellis's bandages come off, my skill as a doctor, on which so much depends, will be laid as bare as Tellis's legs.

The skin is dry and yellow, as if it has never known water. Touching the lines of the bones, I feel a sensation of ice within my chest. The union line is not smooth. There is a knobbly growth where one of the bone ends has over-ridden the other. The second leg is the same as the first.

The bandaging has not been good enough. The bones have joined badly; Tellis will limp, and that limp will be the badge of my limited skill. Hippocrates will not be impressed.

Gloomily, I help Tellis sit on the side of the couch. Cratis and Nicodemus help Tellis to stand; considering his flabby, trembling muscles, he is remarkably steady.

"Very good."

"The splints made it easy for me to walk."

"You fool, Tellis. You have made the bones override." Well, Tellis has finished off my marriage plans for certain.

I have explained why his recovery is so important to me. Tellis has a romantic mind.

"I will do my best for you," he whispers, "but my legs feel like raw bread."

"You stand shorter than you did," says his wife. "Now I can look down on you. That is fitting."

When I let go, I expect Tellis will crash to the floor and break his collar bone.

In the afternoon, Hippocrates comes to see my patient.

"How does it feel, Tellis?" he asks.

"Dreadful," he says, out of habit. Then, remembering his promise, adds, "but improving, thanks to Philo."

Tellis arrives on his feet after a certain amount of undignified heaving. He suppresses his groans; he sacrifices the chance of sympathy.

"Right," says Hippocrates. "Now try to walk."

"Now?" ask Tellis. "Without my splints?"

"Two steps will be sufficient," says Hippocrates.

"Get on with it," I tell him. "Let us get it over."

Tellis takes one step. Then another. And another.

"There is no limp. No limp," I shout at Tellis.

"Wonderful," says Cratis. He smiles. He is indeed a generous fellow.

"Better to break both legs," says Hippocrates, "when the treatment goes wrong."

"Both legs...when treatment..." mutters Cratis, looking for something to write on.

"There is no limp." I look directly at Hippocrates, and the doctor looks steadily back. I am almost certain he smiles. Almost certain.

"There was no agreement."

"I made Tellis my own test, and I believe you saw it as a test, too, though you did not speak of it."

"Had to be certain Lydia approves."

"And what does Lydia say?"

"Happy with any choice of mine. Obedient daughters make obedient wives."

I smile.

"One further impediment."

"I am not rich enough?"

"Lydia should not marry a student. Philo, I declare you a doctor. Gladly."

It is late when I return, full of news and happiness and wine. Mother is near the gate, anxious. But not anxious for me, it seems.

"Xenia has not returned from her flute playing."

"They may have asked her to play some more, she is

very popular."

"She told me which other girls would play there with her. I have seen them walk past on their way home."

"Xenia will be all right. She might even stay the night with the slaves of the house. She did do that once before."

"I think not," says Mother. "She seemed upset when she went out."

"Mother, I am to be married, and you are quite quite safe."

My mother puts her arms around me and I can feel her sobbing.

"It is not just for me is it, Philo?"

"Of course not. I have a bride who will prove me a fine man. What is more, I am a doctor."

"A doctor? My dear son, I am proud. Do you think you should search for Xenia?"

"You do not listen. I am a doctor, and I am to be married. Oh, very well. To please you, I will look for her. But I am sure she is safe."

Xenia is nowhere in the streets. The house where she played the flute is in darkness, the guests returned home. Why look foolish by waking them to ask if our slave is within? That can be the only explanation.

I walk round the streets once more, and my elation ebbs away.

Mother wakes me early. "Do you think she went off with a man? It is the temptation when they play the flute at such parties. A slave Xenia might be, but I love her as my own daughter."

"Xenia can look after herself. She is as tough as a boy."

"Well, I do not know," says Mother, and goes back to the gate to look up the street in the early morning light.

To please her, I go out once more to search for Xenia.

When I get home, Xenia has returned, and waits in the yard. She rushes up to me.

"I have my freedom."

"What have you done?"

"Never mind that. I have bought my freedom from your mother. I am a free woman, and can marry a free man."

"I am pleased for you." I lean forward to kiss her in recognition of her new, sisterly status.

She stands back, only a little.

"Not like that," she says. "Do not kiss me like that."

I look down into her dark oval eyes, which are darting over every feature of my face.

I realise for whom Xenia has bought her freedom, and I know at what price.

"I am betrothed already. To Lydia," I mutter, and try to turn away.

"Philo, it is with me that you laugh. I am your home."

"You have got to understand," I tell her, stepping away. "Please understand."

I go into the house. Like a coward, I cannot turn back and look at her face.

# CHAPTER ELEVEN

She has few belongings and they are wrapped in a large cloth. Xenia looks around the yard as if taking in everything, to hold it to her heart for ever.

"You are going off in a mood," sniffs Agatha. "You will come creeping back tomorrow."

"Do I ever creep?"

I take hold of her shoulders. "Look at me. Going to that house as a nurse is to work as a slave. Here, you are as a daughter. Change your mind, Xenia."

She takes a step back. "My mind is set, Philo. I will live in a huge house and I will play with the children all day. I will be happy as a child myself. Then while they sleep, I shall educate myself. After all, you will have no time to teach me now."

"It takes no time, Xenia, to give you some scrolls to read."

"Besides," Xenia dances away from us towards the gate, "there may be a handsome son who will want to teach me himself."

"You break my heart," says Mother. "I wish I had never given you freedom. But you were so determined that I should."

"You must stay, Xenia," I tell her. "Who else will know things without my telling them?"

"Your wife, perhaps," says Xenia, and bounces out of the gate with her shoulders firm and straight.

\*　　\*　　\*

CHAPTER ELEVEN

My wedding day arrives. Early in the morning, a kingfisher flies over the house, a gaudy flash of blue and orange. "Look," says Agatha. "A sign of fertility in marriage, the kingfisher."

For once I believe her; it is fitting that this excellent marriage should be blessed with children.

Serene is the word in my mind ever afterwards to describe the wedding day. At first light, I walk to the edge of the town and look up into the hills. All the flowers glow on the hillside, the lemon trees and the orchids, and the nodding blue iris; they are flowering for Lydia and myself.

And later, when I walk through the early twilight to the house of Hippocrates, with Nicodemus who comes as my friend in the absence of Timocrates, the air is heavy with the dry smell of almond blossom. It mingles with the dust of the cobbles; I will remember the smell for ever, I know.

"I think," says Nicodemus, "you have chosen a wife who will bring you honour."

"Yes. I shall be envied for her beauty," I agree. "But...I may be stupid...I hope I shall find friendship with her as well."

"That usually lies elsewhere," says Nicodemus, "does it not?"

Lydia looks cooler than ever, her face pale with composure. She does not laugh this evening, but smiles at me with her clear, calm eyes. It is strange she is so certain the marriage will bring contentment.

"I have dedicated my childhood toys to Artemesia," she whispers. "It was my duty, for now I am a woman I have put away childish things." As she leans near to me I can smell the jasmine with which she has been anointed, and the breath of her hair is as fresh as the sea.

Hippocrates stretches out his hands and embraces me warmly. "United already by the art, now bonded through Lydia."

I lead Lydia through the streets to my home by the light of torches, carried by Nicodemus and Cratis. When we reach my house I give her a pomegranate, the gift of fertility. Mother embraces her daughter-in-law, and closes her eyes to lock in tears of happiness. "Such joy for us all," she whispers.

"So long as there are little ones," says Agatha drily. "You look a slip of a girl to me."

When the earth altar has been attended, we are showered with grain and fruit. How else can fertility be guaranteed? I brush the corn from my hair. "Gifts from the goddess to whom my mother dedicated me." I laugh. "A double guarantee."

Lydia picks the grains from her dress; even the gift of the goddess must not fleck her delicate perfection.

Cratis wears the smile of a happy man himself; I cannot remember such a wide, generous smile from Cratis before. I have not realised that Cratis could be perceptive of my feelings.

I look round, wondering if Xenia will come back for the celebration, but she is not here.

The following morning the wedding presents are given. Among them is a fine chair from Nicodemus, and a cedarwood box, inlaid with bronze, from Cratis.

There is a further gift left beside the gate, a small square of wool in which are wrapped five knuckle bones. With them on a scrap of papyrus, the message, "The gift of my childhood. Thank you."

No-one sees this gift arrive, and I, instead of putting

130

it beside the chair and box, hide it at the bottom of my medical bag, where no woman of the house will look. To misunderstand the generosity of this gift or laugh at its simplicity, would be as if to tread on the last butterfly.

It is my bride who organises the new slave girl, Corinna, and it is Lydia who takes joy grinding the flour in the trough, and kneading dough for the bread. She loves to feel it come alive through her skill.

"I would be ashamed to burn the bread," says Lydia, taking golden loaves out of the oven.

"I do not think you will do that," says Mother, and bites her lip, glancing at me.

Lydia's serenity spreads through the house like the warm scent of her baking bread. With relief, Mother relinquishes the tedium of housekeeping and enjoys her new status.

And since I can now ask my own fee, she is not tied to the loom and embroidery all day. She can sit down in the yard, in the shade of the vine, and sometimes even sleep for a while.

In the evenings, I often sit with Lydia under the vine and talk after our meal, wanting her to share the events of the day.

Although no longer students, we remain as a group, sharing the patients and learning from each other.

"Your father talks of us having a centre of our own, a medical school. We might build some rooms on the edge of the town."

"It will save his house being full of herbs," says Lydia. She is working on a small square of embroidery. "By the way, have you noticed?" She points to the corner of the yard.

I glance over to the herb bed which Xenia made. No longer does the pennywort spill over onto the path, nor the sage jostle with the exuberant feverfew. The plants are neatly spaced in three rows, each trimmed to the same size.

"They look tidy," I admit. "Anyway, about the medical school. Hippocrates will not make a decision. And I know why. He still wants the Asclepium. We could never build anything as perfect as that."

"The Fates will decide."

"It is my dream, too, Lydia. Our art is new. We must pass on what we have learned. Without more formality, it is like trying to pass a handful of water from man to man. We need a vessel; a medical school building would contain our art."

Lydia seems to envelop me in her quiet confidence and leans forward to lay her cool hand on mine. "We must wait and see."

"I want you to share my dream, Lydia. That is how I want it to be between us."

Lydia says nothing. She smooths the piece of cloth which she works, smiling gently as she discerns the pattern emerging.

The light from the window is poor. We pull the bed over towards it, and Hippocrates stands so that the best of the light falls on his work. He says, "You understand the risk?"

The woman nods.

"Wait elsewhere. Avoid distress."

"I can comfort him."

"Nicodemus will look after your husband, talk to him, hold him still. And he has had wine and poppy.

You will not be needed," I try to explain.

Nicodemus touches the woman's shoulder. "If Hippocrates says he will cut off my head and put it on back to front, I would let him. Such is my faith in his skill."

The wife agrees to wait in the courtyard.

"We begin," says Hippocrates.

"It may not be an abscess," says Nicodemus again, far from happy. We have discussed the possibility of a tumour at length. Myself, I agree with Hippocrates, that it is an abscess.

"Are you certain?" Nicodemus asks Hippocrates again. "You have always said that it is better not to operate on cancer."

Hippocrates looks for a long time in silence. "Only chance. Poison from abscess will kill."

Nicodemus stands at the man's head, ready to hold him down by the shoulders if he should struggle against the pain. It does not look necessary as he is almost unconscious with the nature of the illness anyway.

Hippocrates takes the first knife, long, with a point, and makes the incision, over the hard swelling in the stomach.

I hand him sheep's wool to stem the flow of blood, and wool strips to wipe out the cavity that reveals itself.

"Small knife. The sharpest," mutters Hippocrates as he prods at the growth. "Let us find out."

He cuts. The pus spurts everywhere and, when the pressure is gone, it pours from the swelling as if from a bottomless well.

Hippocrates smiles briefly. "Abscess."

Relief floods in, as always. We have taken a

calculated risk. We have made a decision out of our own knowledge. We are proved right.

When the abscess is drained, we wash it out with wine, and put a dressing over the wound.

From the door I call, "Your husband is a lucky man, it is not a growth."

"Apollo be praised," she says, and sinks to her knees, arms stretched to the sky.

I tell Lydia, "I nearly said, 'Not Apollo, but Hippocrates.' If he had not been so certain of his diagnosis, he would have done nothing."

"He did his duty as a doctor," says Lydia.

"But do you not see, to have the knowledge, to know what is happening out of sight, is wonderful. It is your father who has discovered so much."

Lydia smiles as if she is a little amused at my enthusiasm.

Fleetingly, I wonder if she is not my chattel, but that I belong to Lydia; that I am merely a replacement in her life for Hippocrates. I would love to know Xenia's opinion.

"Have you seen how tight the skin lies on Lydia's cheek bones?" asks Hippocrates, smiling at me.

I frown, not understanding.

"Quite soon," says Hippocrates, "you will realise."

"I am certain now, Philo," says Lydia. "I had to be certain before I told you."

"Certain of what?"

She says nothing but smiles at me. Added to her serenity is an inner satisfaction. Now the truth begins to dawn.

"When will it be born?"

"Not it. He. Not long before the almond is in flower again."

"Anyone else would say the spring. You have to make it even more beautiful."

"A beautiful son, who will be like you and my father," she says. "Are you pleased with me?"

I sigh. All the world will acknowledge that I cannot be such a plain man after all, with such a beautiful wife. Even more certain if I am the father of a fine son.

As she grows bigger, her face becomes even more lovely, as if to distract the eye. Agatha ignores her beauty. "You are a frail mite," she says. "I only hope you do not have a bad time."

"Everything will be easy," says Lydia, smiling at her.

Agatha looks tartly down her nose. "I would not call those good child-bearing hips myself."

"Be quiet, Agatha." I turn to Lydia. "Agatha can be bitter. There is no truth in her words. You must take no notice."

She smiles radiantly at me, with no trace of distress in her summer-sea eyes. "My path will be smooth."

Mother puts her arms round Lydia, and hugs her. "What a happy family we will all be. I wonder if I can find the little swing your father hung from the vine when you were small, Philo?"

"Or perhaps a new one?" suggests Lydia.

She sits in the weaving room in the day-time and with me in the evenings, sewing soft wool garments for the child, and later she embroiders a shawl in which to wrap the baby at birth.

"I wonder how Timocrates is doing?" I reflect one

evening. "In the market place the news of the war is not good. Sometimes I look out to sea and imagine I can see the boat from Athens coming towards the island. Even though I know we will have the news long before the men."

"He will be fine," says Lydia. "He will come home soon." She smiles, wonderfully serene. She smooths out her work on her knee and picks from it an invisible speck of dust.

"You cannot know that," I say, frowning at her.

Lydia smiles. "Would you pass me the blue thread, please?"

It is her deep goodness that makes her believe all things are possible. And especially for Timocrates.

Agatha is out early. She comes in now, red-faced with excitement and anger. "News of Sicily comes in with the wine from Samos. The war is nearly lost," she says. "They say the Athenians are retreating. They are no match for the Sicilians."

"That is bad. On the other hand, it might mean that Timocrates will come home soon."

Although Lydia turns more and more inwards, towards her own warm world, she does go out once to buy some pottery.

"Today, I saw someone who used to live here," she tells me. "Your mother's slave girl, I think. Xenia, yes, that is her name."

"She bought her freedom," I explain, and wish Xenia's presence had not intruded into the peace of the evening.

"She was very quiet," says Lydia. "Not laughing like she used to. I remember seeing her in the market once, when my father took me to look at his plane tree."

"Quiet?"

"But she was so polite to me, and says she is pleased about the baby. Then she came to the house later with a little gift. Look." Lydia holds up a tiny wool cloak, with a woven border of blue harebells. The flowers are not all the same shape.

"Did she look happy?"

"Why do you ask?"

I can only tell half the truth. "She might have been missing us all."

Lydia says eventually, "Xenia looks wistful. Yes, she looks very wistful."

"She is probably all right." I try to cultivate Lydia's contented vision. I would like to have known for myself, all the same, that Xenia is well.

Lydia leans back in her chair. Her breathing is quite shallow these days.

"Dear Lydia, are you very tired?"

"My legs are a bit heavy, that is all. Everything is fine. Soon I shall give my husband a beautiful son."

"I do not think you should go out any more." The exercise might make her tired and, besides, I am left with an inexplicable feeling over those messy harebells.

Some days later, Mother has more surprising news than any from over the water.

"Philo, Xenia is no longer a nurse at the big house. The mistress dismissed her because the master paid Xenia too much attention."

"So she will come back here?"

"She is going to be married, Philo. Tomorrow."

"Married? Whoever to?"

"To Cratis."

"Cratis?"

"But she will leave for her marriage from this house. As my daughter. It is the least I can do for her."

"She cannot marry *Cratis*, he is too dull. She cannot possibly marry Cratis."

"She will be happy to marry a doctor," says Lydia. "You should be proud, for she was not born free. Cratis is a good doctor, surely?"

"He is not good enough for Xenia."

There is a question in Lydia's eyes as she picks up her sewing again. "I consider Xenia to be most fortunate."

Where my marriage day was serene, Xenia's is joyful; she takes care to make it so. Mother, too, for she has woven into some white linen for the bridal robe, the palest stripe of lemon at the hem, dyed from the saffron crocus. Down the length of the arms, the material is caught together with tiny silver brooches in the shape of petals. They are the ones Mother wore at her own wedding.

Xenia's eyes are so wide and dark that I wonder if she has trickled in belladonna. Or is it emotion that dilates the pupils so strangely? I hope it may be happiness.

"Let me tidy your hair." Lydia generously pins back strands of Xenia's hair escaping from her head band of flowers.

Cratis comes to lead her to his house, and as she leaves with him, she glances across the room to catch my eye. Then she laughs up at Cratis, showing him joy and fun and warmth; she touches his arm.

Cratis coughs and smiles self-consciously back.

Xenia walks away to the house of Cratis on the far side of the town and, from now on, it will be *her* slave, not Xenia, who will shop in the market place. Nicodemus and I carry the torches.

"I am a little surprised," admits Nicodemus quietly, "that Cratis should marry a freed slave. It is not what I would have expected."

"He is the lucky one. Xenia is...well, Xenia is such a special person."

Nicodemus glances at me, with only the merest hint of his old arrogance.

Cratis mislays the pomegranate and has to make do with an orange to hand his bride on her arrival.

The pair are showered with grains and rice. Cratis gets an oat in his eye, and stands with one side of his face all squeezed up, a tear trickling down his cheek. Xenia teases the oat out of his eye with the sleeve of her dress. Gently she squeezes his arm and smiles at him to make him laugh at himself. Cratis almost manages it.

The smoke spiralling from the altar in the sacrifice to Aphrodite seems strangely heavy; it does not waft up easily in the night air. In my heart, I know why.

The news is all round the market. A fisherman off the boat from Athens brought it early this morning.

"Dead," says Hippocrates. "By a javelin. Why Timocrates?" He sits down and puts his head in his hands.

"Are you certain?"

"When he was struck, he went down like a stone. The witness is certain he is dead."

· It is as if a spectre has been following me, which now dances into reality before my eyes. Always, I have known this could happen, and always have I kept it out of sight.

We all who have been students together talk long of his prowess, and of his beauty and his strong spirit. By remembering him fondly, we pay tribute as if at the funeral we will not attend; the funeral he will never have.

His death is different from that of a patient. It is outside our help, in the hand of Atropos alone. I had begun to forget the cruel whims of the gods.

As a result, death seems everywhere. The sky feels heavy as if before an earthquake. The island has not felt the wrath of Poseidon for many years now, but in the gloom, I almost feel the presentiment of the god's anger coming again.

Because Timocrates was my friend, I visit his mother. She sits staring across the small room in which she lives.

"What can I say to you? We will all miss him so much, but especially me," I tell her, "because of our rivalry."

She does not look at me. "I have forgiven him, you know."

"Forgiven him for what?"

Now she turns. "Do you not know?"

I have a suspicion, something else which I have never allowed to surface in my mind.

"He stole it, you know. Stole my necklace."

"I did not know."

"Look." She goes to a small chest and opens it. Under everything else, hidden against thieves, is Timocrates' crown of wild olive, dried and yellow. "When he gave it to me, he cried for my forgiveness."

"It meant so much to be able to go to Olympia."

"I am glad. Emeralds were not the gift of love, I

realise now. This is better. Leaves are living and they grow. Did grow."

I creep away as she hides the wreath once more from the world, for safety.

I have not even reached the market when Agatha comes running up the street.

"Come quickly," she says. "It is Lydia." She shakes her head and puts an ominously consoling hand on my shoulder.

I brush her aside, and race back to the house.

Lydia is lying on her couch; Mother is beside her with a firm, determined smile on her face, a smile I have seen before.

Lydia whispers, "The baby will belong to this day; I feel it." Her face is no longer serene; there are lines under the eyes like threads puckered in smooth silk.

I take her hand. "It is not your time yet. You must rest." Her hand is cold in mine, and damp.

"It is for you, Philo. Tell me I am a good wife."

"For us, Lydia, my perfect wife."

Towards midday, Agatha goes for Dorcas, the midwife. Even now all might be well, but there is disharmony with nature. The baby is eager; the mother reluctant. Heat fights with cold. Winter is mistaken for the spring.

"She has the fever," says Dorcas, her arms red and muscular like a man's. "The body does not work for the baby as it should, but the baby is determined. It cannot be held back. We should give a draught of ergot."

Hippocrates stays her. "You are a fine midwife, Dorcas, but be subtle, I beg you. Ergot is too strong. The baby must not come fast."

Lydia's eyes are closed as if she sleeps. From time to

time the contractions waken her, and she falls back, limp after each spasm.

At last the midwife says, "The baby is coming."

We wait outside while Lydia lies passive, her body making the delivery on its own, without her conscious help.

A doctor's experience of childbirth is nothing to that of Dorcas, but we feel helpless beyond that. A patient in pain, Hippocrates knows instinctively how to help, but helping his daughter in this state is outside all his skill. Her passivity frightens us. The frailty of her spirit engulfs us.

All day we wait, and Agatha lights the charcoal braziers against the cold.

From within the room, the midwife shouts out, "It lives. The little scrap is alive."

I feel as if I am washed up on a beach, no longer punished by the waves.

Dorcas brings the baby out to Mother, wrapped in a piece of linen. I look down at my son.

While I go to Lydia, my mother washes the baby and warms him with woollen cloths, wrapping him in the shawl Lydia has embroidered. "A fine boy. Thin, but what a well-shaped head," she murmurs.

"Lydia," I say. She lies without waking, sweat trickling from her forehead.

"We have a son."

Her eyelids flicker. "I am pleased for you."

"The fever is running high," says Dorcas. "There is little we can do." She glances at Hippocrates and slips away without asking for her money.

"What must we do?" I ask.

"I cannot give a prognosis. My heart disagrees with my mind."

"A sacrifice at the temple," I suggest, "though I fear to leave her?"

"Stay," says Hippocrates. "Never be tempted to confuse the work of man with that of the gods. Apollo and Asclepius are quite capable of reading a man's heart. They are above flattery and supplication."

"Should we let blood?" I ask, clutching at any idea.

"Sponge her face. Hold her hand. Talk gently to her," says Hippocrates.

"Will she be all right?"

"We do not know all the skill of medicine yet," he says, and the words are pessimistic.

"Come on, Lydia. You must fight to live."

Again, the pale eyes flicker over my face. "No... strength."

"Find strength, Lydia."

There is no answer.

Such fever rages within Lydia that the balance should be restored quite easily; such love surrounding her should bring harmony to the fraught body. But neither heat nor love can win.

Through the small hours of the night we sit, and the fever rages. Lydia turns and tosses, throws off her sheet, claws it to her again, unconscious to the world. Too soon, the crisis comes.

With the same gentle acceptance she has always shown, Lydia allows the life force to drift from her, with one brief, quivering sigh. Lydia dies on the second day of her fever.

"Lydia," I shout, and would have shaken those still shoulders to wake her again to life.

Hippocrates holds me back, and it is the sight of his tears which bring me to the truth.

"Your mother will attend," Hippocrates says quietly,

and leads me outside.

While Mother does what she must in Lydia's room, and then what she can to comfort myself and Hippocrates, it is Agatha who finds a wet nurse for the baby. And it is Agatha who cradles the child for the whole of his first night, keeps him warm with shawls, as he yells his dislike for this frost-cruel world into which he has come unwelcome and before his time.

# CHAPTER TWELVE

"He should be called by his own name," says Mother.

"Lydia wanted the name to be Leon."

"He will be Leon, then?"

"What does it matter?"

I sit in the yard of Hippocrates' house. If I wait long enough and never take my eyes off the door of the spinning room, Lydia might come out to me. Sometimes I close my eyes and doze, for all the time I feel tired. Then she does come through the door. But she turns white and runs away. When I wake up, I feel worse.

Hippocrates does not lecture for many days. He lies on his bed staring at nothing. When he returns to his patients he is an older man.

"Persevere," he tells me. "And think of Leon."

"I am no use to him. Leon needs a mother. A baby does not need a father, only those who will feed and clean him."

"What about love?"

"Love to a baby is being warm and not being hungry. Anyway, how can I be expected to love that swathed bundle which caused Lydia's death?"

Winter is so cold that the men who live in the mountains have come down to the town for shelter. Is the season chasing false gems, the diamonds which seem to glint in the snow as the torchlight catches them. I remember my beautiful wife whose hands were as cool as the dew, whose brow was as smooth as the clean washed sand, in whose care my whole future had securely lain.

The swallows come, and Arcturus, so bright, rises in the evening sky and can be seen all of the night.

It is Agatha, not Mother, who cares for Leon. I had supposed Mother would look after the child. That she does not is an act of generosity. She watches Agatha rock the small child in her arms, does and says nothing.

Ever since that first night, when the slip of life was linked so frailly with the world, when, at any moment, he might have chosen to whisper back to his mother, Agatha wills her confidence into him; determines the lungs to breathe, the mouth to take milk. There is a naturalness between them and Leon's first relationship is forged out of necessity.

It is Agatha who dilutes the goat's milk to supplement that from the wet nurse. It is Agatha who prepares the first light gruel. And it is to Agatha that Leon gives his first smile.

Once I see Xenia on her way to the fountain house. She says simply, "I prayed to Apollo when I heard that Lydia was ill. I hoped with my whole heart that she would be well again."

"You do not believe in the gods."

"I have learned there is more than endeavour. I thought all things were possible with determination. But they are not. What else is necessary I have not discovered. So I gave Apollo the chance to show that it is him."

There is something missing from Xenia's eyes. It is joy. And her mouth, wide and generous as ever, is no longer on the brink of laughing.

"You are...happy?" I ask.

Xenia smiles. "I shall pray that tranquillity may soon return to you." She takes up her pitcher of water, nods to her own slave to bring her pitcher, too, and walks slowly on her way.

Flowers come again to the hillside. They come to mock me. "Why did you not hold Lydia to her time?" I shout as I pace through the hills above the town. I trample on every bog iris I can see, crush the anemones, kick the orchid heads. She might have been here still, if they had.

"You. You mask of Demeter, with your paper spring. Oh goddess, you may really call yourself great, if spring ever comes to me again."

But the gods have beaten me down. They have punished me for hubris. And because I lack excellence as a citizen. Like my father, I have neglected the pursuit of politics.

I have some bad nights. Once I go out into the yard and look up at the sky, transfixed.

The moon is chipped; a bite has been taken out of one edge of the glowing disc of Artemis. And as I watch, the whole moon gradually disappears.

The yard is black, the night shadows merge into one obscuring blanket. Slowly, another moon emerges, piece by piece, and eventually the night is as it has always been.

It is a further sign, this eclipse, of the great powers' displeasure.

I cannot stay the moon. And I cannot bring Lydia back.

The news comes from the market place that Athens is defeated. The enemy came by night, while our men slept, and the camp was captured. They might have withdrawn to safety, but the moon was eclipsed, and Nicias would not give the order to march until they had tarried thrice nine days on the advice of a woman of much wisdom. I knew that moon meant no good.

It is summer when tragedy hovers over us again. Agatha's condition starts with a sore throat, and soon she is coughing and spluttering like an old man. Mother takes over caring for Leon. Agatha lies on her couch, grey and breathless, eating only figs and bread and drinking more wine than is good for her.

"Pneumonia," I tell her gently. "But you will recover. We can predict the critical days and act accordingly. Today is the third day of your illness."

This third day, the crisis will come. If Agatha rallies, her chances are good.

"You should eat less food, and take less wine."

"You are not starving me to death," says Agatha, showing stubborn spirit.

"Soup then."

"I must keep my strength. I will eat what I please."

"Thick soup." I leave it at that.

Agatha's own obstinacy should carry her through the disease easily. But Agatha reads the signs. "In this house," she says, "death. Death goes in threes. Your father. Lydia. Now me."

"Superstition. Agatha, superstition has ruled your life. Do not let it kill you."

Agatha closes her eyes, and lies back. "The light has gone out of me." The lids of her closed eyes are red and veined, the skin below them quite blue.

As the day draws on, Agatha falls back. Her eyes have hollow sockets and she is restless, sitting up and throwing herself down. Her breathing is crackly, the forehead hot to touch.

By the following morning, she has sunk into a delirium, only wafting occasionally back to awareness.

I sponge her face and arms. Her breathing is like air forced through a heap of wet leaves. Sometimes she nearly chokes with a painful cough.

Mother, leaving Leon sleeping, comes into the room. "He is asleep at last, but I lack Agatha's way with him."

"Sit with us. We need your willpower, Mother."

"What shall we do for her? Surely Delphia has infusions to break that cough. Come along Philo, surely you can help her."

"Only the body can fight the disease. See how the heat created in her is trying to restore the balance?"

"Poor Agatha," says Mother. "An old fighting horse like her will not go down. Will she, Philo?"

I cannot answer.

"Will she, Philo?"

"I do not know."

"Death. Is there nothing but death in this house? Have we not seen enough of it?"

"Stay with me please, Mother. We will see the crisis through together."

Agatha stirs from time to time, sometimes she opens her eyes, but she does not see.

I look at the tart old lady and remember another face ill upon a pillow.

Corinna, the slave girl, comes running in. "That baby. He is crying again. There is nothing I can do to stop him."

"I will come in a minute," says Mother.

Agatha will not rouse herself. The breathing is shallow now; her eyes are thin white slits.

"A bad sign," says Mother.

"Bring Leon in," I say suddenly. "Bring him to the door, while he is making all that noise."

The sharp, furious cries come nearer; Leon is outraged that he is not comforted by Agatha. His world, once more, is bleak.

Agatha's lids close over the white slits, and then they open properly, the pupils struggling to focus. She turns towards the noise in the doorway.

She mouths something.

"Listen to Leon, Agatha." I lean over her. "Hear him crying? He needs you." The eyes open wider, and the pupils hold steady.

Agatha tries to stretch out her hand, but it falls back. "Hush, Leon," she murmurs. "Agatha is here."

I wave at Corinna to take Leon away out of hearing. Mother goes after her.

"Leon has stopped crying. You have comforted him. He sleeps. Do not go away. He will want you again when he wakes. You sleep now, Agatha, while he sleeps."

She nods, as if understanding. She closes her eyes properly and the breathing is easier.

Within an hour, the fever leaves her and she sleeps peacefully.

"The crisis has passed," says Mother. She smiles at me. "You showed her she is needed."

Yes. I recognise my own powers now, powers which

150

come from knowledge and perception. I have helped
Agatha when the gods would not.

In the hills beyond the town, I can be alone. Below,
Astipalea sits white in the dust; and beyond it, like the
beaten bronze of Lydia's hand mirror, gleams the
sea.

Out in the distance, the island of Nissiros, the great
rock thrown by Poseidon, still rumbles with the rage of
the god; smoke whimpers from its tall hill.

I lie on the grass with the sun on my face, tired
enough to sleep now. But instead of sleep come scenes
to haunt me again.

Lydia, with her doll, as a child; Lydia in her wedding
beauty; Lydia baking bread, her face radiant with
fulfilment.

It begins to comfort me to think about her; there is
less sting.

But I can only remember how she looked; not how
she was. I can remember so little of her mind; I can
remember nothing we shared absolutely together. I
knew of no window into her soul. Now, I might as well
try to trap a butterfly's wing, and look at it each day
until it powders to nothing.

And I wonder how much ever was real. Or was it all
only in my mind?

At last, I know this tender, dragonfly dream will not
sustain me for ever.

Slowly, I set off to the town. Then, I walk more
quickly until I am running. I want to see Leon. If the
child sleeps, I will wake him up. If he sits on Agatha's
knee, I will sweep him off. I will hug him. I will talk
to him.

The time has come for me to get to know my son.

As Agatha recovers, we sometimes pull her couch out into the yard so that she can rest under the vine. The year has turned, and there is softness in the air. She nurses Leon, who always sleeps so much more peacefully in her arms than anywhere else.

"One day, Philo, you will be healed yourself."

"Unlike you to be so comforting."

"I may have been a little sharp on occasions," she admits.

I pull a face of mock disbelief.

"It may be hard to understand," says Agatha, "but when you do not love, you can be very unhappy. No man asked my father to draw up a marriage contract for me, you know. But now I have seen you suffer more than I ever did." She looks down at Leon. "In my old age, Philo, I have learned to give. I am some use at last."

"You saved Leon on that first dreadful night. He would have slipped away, too, if it had not been for you."

"I can spot a fine lad. Lucky not to get his looks from his father, I tell him."

"Now I know you are cured."

When the blossoms appear, and the iris smudges the hills with blue, I am lonely but no longer want to trample the flowers down with rage. A year is a measured space, a marked-off period.

As I leave home after the morning meal, I see Xenia walking along the street, coming from visiting a sick kinswoman, a relative of Cratis. It is many moons since I last saw her.

Perhaps because I see her as my sister, I say, "Come and sit down in the yard. Tell me how you are getting along."

Xenia glances round to see there is no-one in the street before coming hesitantly back into her old home. We sit down under the vine, and I offer her some refreshment, but she shakes her head.

"So you are a lady of leisure?"

"Indeed I am not," she says, a little flicker of the old fire springing up. "I have taught myself to read much more fluently. Well, Cratis taught me really. It is an accomplishment that not all Greek women have, even though they have been free all their lives."

I laugh. "Is reading part of your great plan of freedom?"

"You know that."

"So Cratis is proud of you?"

"Well, he does not say."

"I am proud of you." I take her hands as I would a sister's. "Our little Xenia doing so well. But are you happy? Is your life really what you hoped for?"

"Of course it is." She laughs emphatically and stares down at the table.

Eventually, she lifts her head and we each look into the face of the other.

At last she whispers, "I may have been a slave, but as children we were true friends. You know me better than I know myself. You have no need to ask that question."

"There is much we never need to say."

Xenia frees her hands and stands up to go, smiling at me with her old smile, teasing, taunting, sadness gone. "I shall keep today in my heart."

With her dark hair now in a sophisticated braid and a blue cloak draped elegantly round her shoulders, Xenia looks different, yet strangely, she seems to have changed not at all.

Once she was as a sister; now I will never think of her as a sister again.

"Xenia," cries Mother coming out of the spinning room. "How good to see you, and how elegant you are now."

"Quite the lady," says Agatha, following. But she bites her lip and adds, "As pretty as ever."

"I have visited a sick relative, and am rewarded by seeing you all again."

Agatha fetches Leon and gives him to Xenia to hold. Together, the old face and the young lean over the sleeping child cradled in Xenia's arms.

"He is beautiful," she says.

"Like his mother," says Agatha.

"Like his mother," says Xenia. "Truly beautiful."

"But you have no child," comments Agatha.

"No."

"Ah," says Agatha, sounding wise. "Now, the eagle finds it difficult to lay eggs. But if the bird will put a stone in its nest, thereafter it has no problem. If a woman can find this very stone, she will conceive."

"Agatha, you never change. All this superstition, when you have a doctor in the family."

"There is wisdom in the old beliefs," says Agatha.

"I am not walking in the hills looking for an eagle's nest," says Xenia. She leaves, the scent of jasmine lingering; she need not now perfume only one foot.

Without realising why, I begin to make a habit of passing the fountain house. The time seems to coincide with when Xenia fetches the water. Or I walk where she might pass to visit her kinswoman. Sometimes it means taking an indirect route to a patient's house.

Once I see her and we speak carefully of the weather and the war. For five days after that, I deliberately avoid the fountain house. Then pretending to myself that I have to make the calls in a particular order, I pass the place once more where the women carry their pitchers to collect the best spring water of the town.

After that, I see Xenia three mornings out of four.

"Good morning, Xenia." I try to sound surprised.

"You walk this way a great deal, Philo."

"I am visiting a patient with a prolonged complaint. Very prolonged."

"Cratis will not discuss his patients," says Xenia wistfully, "but I love to hear about people. Little stories like you used to bring home."

"Cratis is right," I tell her quickly. "I should not mention patients either. It is...well...I used to tell you."

"There is no reason, now."


Flowers of the spring are everywhere, the creamy wallflowers in the rocks, and the periwinkle under foot, while the hills are pink with thyme. Demeter, you spent one whole summer underground and now you have come late in the year. I can scarcely believe what the goddess whispers to me on the wind.

The delicate fire of friendship responds sensitively to the contrary winds of absence. Too great a gale will puff out a flicker; too faint a breeze, and the flame will sink back into the wood and die.

By seeing and avoiding, I come to recognise what Xenia has always known. But having deliberately kindled the fire, I try to pretend that it does not burn.

Besides, I cannot steal another doctor's wife,

especially if that doctor is Cratis.

Lydia's face, in my mind, becomes a painting; easier to see, but further removed from reality. One night I dream that we sit together at dinner, and on the table between us lies a golden apple. I do not take the fruit and neither does she. Gradually, each of us begins to crumble to dust, until we finally disappear; only the apple remains, golden, but untouched.

One day, Cratis comes to see a patient with me. Nicodemus is talking about Menon, as he often does, and says casually, "You do not mention if you have a child, Cratis."

"It does not seem as if I will," says Cratis, not taking his eyes from the wound he is examining.

"A woman needs a child," says Nicodemus. "Does your wife not tell you that?"

"It is not something we discuss," says Cratis primly.

"Perhaps it should be," I mutter.

"Xenia wants for nothing," says Cratis. "So she is happy."

I remember how Xenia described love, and I know there are no lighted windows between her and Cratis. I remember how Xenia saw into all our hearts when she was a slave. The walls around her now are blank and cold. Only when Xenia was a baby and I learned about exposure on the hillside, did I ever feel she needed help. Until now.

A week later I see her again. "Will you come and visit my mother? She was so happy to see you before. Perhaps tomorrow afternoon?"

"Women should not desire to look beyond the home, but to see your mother again, well, that would be understandable. Will you be there?"

"That will depend on my patients, not me.

Tomorrow afternoon then."

The day is important. Tomorrow, my mother has already told Agatha that they will visit her own sister in the next village.

I wait in the house on the following afternoon. I visit the barber in the morning, and my hair looks rather neat. I lay out wine and sweetmeats in the dining room.

I make my decision. Xenia must choose between Cratis and myself. Divorce might be unusual, but it is not difficult.

Time passes slowly as I pace round the yard waiting to hear the soft footsteps in the road beyond.

At last Xenia stands at the gate.

"I know your mother and Agatha are not here," she says. "I saw them leave the town earlier today." She wears a stole round her face like a matron, and speaks in a flat, tired voice.

"But you came here all the same." I run forward. "I knew you would. Xenia, there is so much to talk about though we scarcely need speak."

Xenia takes a step backwards. "I know what you will say today," she says. "And I have already considered the answer."

"I want nothing dishonourable," I tell her quickly, wondering if she thinks I only want furtive meetings and deceit. "I will speak to Cratis myself."

"The answer," says Xenia clearly, "is that you and I cannot meet again." She looks me straight in the face, and I know she has prepared her words.

"That is not what you want."

"I bought my freedom to be a true woman, not an adulteress. What manner of person would desert

Cratis, who has always been faithful to me? I would be less than a slave."

"The times we met were not by accident. That must have told you where the path would lead."

"I chose not to consider," says Xenia, "because such moments were dear. But now I see it will defile us both, you as a doctor and me as a woman."

"Cratis does not deserve you. You are so alive. His spirit is already dead."

"Cratis may be dull, but he loved me when I was a slave. He married me with no dowry, against the wishes of his father. He loved me when you did not."

"Why did you marry him, Xenia?"

"Because I could not remain in the house where Lydia was your bride. Cratis was the only place for me to go."

"All the more reason now..."

"All the less reason, Philo." She glances at the gate. "Wait."

She walks straight out of the yard, and does not look back. And there is in her step that bounce of pride she discovered as a child in slavery.

Life is bleak, but the pain is not for myself. I watch Agatha holding Leon, the child alert still in the hour before sleep, the old wrinkled face laughing tenderly down at the round smiling boy, with the stretching fingers and the bedribbled chin.

Should Leon be laughing up into those crinkled cheeks? Should that dried skin be his best-loved face? Not when that face should have been Lydia's. Not when that smile might have been...

Agatha looks up. "I know what you think," she says, gently for Agatha. "If you ever do find a mother for this little one, I will not cling to him, I promise you. I love him too much."

"Agatha." I cannot stop myself crying.

Absently, she pats my hand. "Old Agatha has learned to give in her grumpy old age. I am lucky, you know, to have learned at all."

This night, I make a sacrifice on the small hearth altar in the yard to Hestia, goddess of the home. I pour a libation of wine into the earth, and roast a cockerel on the hearth.

I pray before it and watch the smoke pour up, up into the night air. It seems to waft right up to the stars.

"Goddess of all life in the home, I make this sacrifice to beseech you to restore to my son, Leon, all that which he has lost and for which he will one day crave."

Apollo did not listen to Xenia when she prayed at Leon's birth for his mother. Demeter denied Lydia the spring. But this night, it seems, Hestia hears me as I pray alone in the dark.

# CHAPTER THIRTEEN

It is hot, even for our island. Three of us secure the patient, while Hippocrates cauterises the painful hip. The smell of scorched flesh is revolting. The rod dies from white to scarlet, through grey to black. Sweat runs off our noses, and plops on the floor. Cratis's wet hands skid on the patient's leg. Nicodemus, red as a tomato, head tipped back, eyes closed, heaves to restrain the patient.

When work is finished, Hippocrates says, "We must get cool. We will go to the forest."

He brings a basket of fruit, and Nicodemus thoughtfully loads up with a jar of wine.

The air is still, as if in waiting. Sometimes it is so before a storm, but there are no spiralling clouds in the sky, nothing to break the dazzling ceiling of the world; nothing to clear the humid blanket which lies across the hills.

We find a spot to rest in the fringe of the trees, from where we can look down on Astipalea and over the sea towards Nissiros. The air is strangely silent; not a single bird is singing.

I lie back, head on a cushion of pine needles and eat another fig. Hippocrates cools his forehead with some wine. Cratis sees how far he can spit cherry stones.

Nicodemus blows time away on a dandelion clock. "Have you heard what is said of the Asclepium?"

"What?" Cratis eats the last cherry.

"Half-empty."

"We win the argument." Hippocrates smiles.

"Because there is less work to do, priests are leaving for the mainland."

Hippocrates nods. "Inevitable."

"Great Poseidon," says Cratis, suddenly standing up. "Whatever is that?"

He points to the sea and we follow his accusing finger.

Far out across the dark water is a wave, a solitary white-topped monster, rolling into the shore, fast, like fire over oil. We stand up to watch.

Now comes the noise, the rumbling, which gives voice to the shifting of the earth. The sky roars with the rocks and the sea. It is suddenly dark and the gods rage.

The juddering earth throws us to the ground. The clamour of bubbling and boiling and thunder increases. It drowns our shouts.

"Earthquake," bellows Nicodemus. "Get away from the trees." He begins to crawl towards the open ground, fighting against the heaving earth. Seeing, not hearing, we follow.

The trees smash down behind us, snapping weak as straw while others uproot.

How long the rumbling and earth-shaking lasts, I cannot say, but the wrath, even of Poseidon, does not last for ever. The ground moves less violently, slips more reluctantly, and now, at last, all anger dies away.

We can stand up.

"Run," says Hippocrates, and starts down the hill.

Below us, the rising dust hides the town. As we draw near, we see the rubble of the houses through the white cloud and hear the screams of the women yelling for their children. Grey figures burrow desperately into heaps of stones. One woman lies weeping over her discovery.

Alexander rushes across the road. "My sacks are burst open. The dust is as thick as the flour. I am ruined."

Menon runs up the street, his limp exaggerated by effort. "Mother is stuck in the house."

"Is she hurt?"

"She cannot get out."

Nicodemus races on.

Choking now with dust, I stumble to our house. But it is no longer a house. Like everything else, it is a pile of stones not as high as my shoulder.

In panic, I scramble over the wreckage. "Leon. Mother. *LEON*!"

There is no sound. I drag at the stones, trying to tug them away, but they are too heavy to move. Besides, I must not dislodge any, in case Leon is buried underneath.

"Philo." Cratis appears at the gap where the gate was. "Your mother is helping in the next street. The child is with her and the old lady." He dashes away.

Already the injured are lying in the street, away from the rubble which might collapse further. Mother is comforting the crying, tearing her cloak into strips to bandage bleeding wounds, re-uniting children with their parents, calming the frightened.

"It is all over now," she keeps saying. "You are alive. The earthquake is finished." She glances over her shoulder as if she is looking for someone. She sees me. Mother, Leon and I all hug one another, half laughing, half crying.

"I was grinding the corn," she whispers, "the gift of

162

Demeter. So I was in the yard. Leon was with me. We had time to get out. She gave us her protection, Philo, I know it."

"Mother, I must get to work."

"Of course. It will be a long day. I will bring you some food later, if there is any to be had."

"Went all dark," says Leon, tugging at my tunic.

Holding him close, I whisper, "Nothing will ever go wrong again, I promise."

Nicodemus is a good organiser.

"Will the women collect every blanket. Also clothes suitable for making bandages. The men carry as many injured as possible to the market place so we can treat them more quickly. Bion, find a source of clean water, and fill any pot there is left."

We work with tears in our eyes, looking on bleeding wounds, on paralysed legs, on death.

"Be my runner," I say to Tellis. He is unhurt, having been asleep in an olive grove at the time. "Find me henbane if you can, and dressings. Try Hippocrates' house. There will be medicine buried somewhere. Try to find Delphia if she is still alive."

"Oh, oh," says Tellis. "'It is terrible. Oh, Philo, is it not terrible? Great gods, have mercy."

"Just get on with it."

He waddles off on his misshapen legs.

A child runs by screaming, terrified because his mother will not wake up. The screams are heard. Xenia gathers the child up in her arms, as she leads another small boy to his father. Delphia, shivering with fear, hobbles up and thrusts her herbs upon us.

Anaxion is trapped beneath his door lintel, which is jammed by precariously balanced stones. His legs stick out, and blood runs onto the road.

"The stones must be moved one at a time. Otherwise he will be crushed," says Cratis.

"I will find strong men from the foundry. I must be quick, or he will bleed to death."

When I return with men strong enough to shift the stones, there are four legs sticking out into the road. Cratis has wriggled in beside him. The bleeding has stopped.

"You fool, Cratis. You could have been crushed yourself."

The foundry men get the two out.

"Unconscious. Bleeding from the chest. Be dead by now, if I had not stopped the wound with wool," says Cratis.

"He owes his life to you." I am warmed by Cratis's courage. He says nothing, but there is a rare satisfaction in his half-smile.

Agatha cuts up vegetables to make soup for the many, over a fire in the street. "Mark my words," she says. "Troubles never come alone."

The wrath of Poseidon is quickly spent, and he is sunny again. Afterwards the god is forgiven, for he has always been volatile.

But man can cause misery with none of the magnificent power that belongs to the great one; he who rules over the domain of the sea. Man can heap misery on misery, as we discover, when two days later the Spartan fleet sails into the harbour of Astipalea.

The ships are on their way to Asia to find shelter, but the men come ashore at Cos first on small rafts.

Men run down gratefully to the harbour at the sight of them. "Have you brought supplies?"

The Spartans push past and go ahead to the ruins of

the town, led by Antyochos, whose face is scarred with cruelty.

"We are devastated," says a member of the council. "If you cannot help, then please leave. We cannot accommodate you."

"Servants of Athens," sneers the Spartan leader. "We take our due." He spots a pile of possessions, chipped pots and a few clothes, the fruit from hours of digging. He rifles through them, searching for jewellery.

"Get out, you dogs," says Nicodemus. "We have trouble enough."

Antyochos knocks him to the ground, and the Spartans move on to collect two silver jugs.

They loot the whole town, stealing jewellery, food, sheep, and women, even a set of surgical instruments.

"Go into the hills with Leon," I tell Mother. "The town is in ruins, but I believe several villages still stand."

Many of the women and children go up to the hill villages, clambering over the rock paths by night, seeking shelter from strangers.

Some families leave our island of sorrows for good, sailing west to another small island, which we later hear they call Astipalea, after our town.

One Spartan soldier, as he plunders a house near the temple of Apollo, dislodges some rubble which crushes a bone in his back. Friends bring him to Hippocrates as he treats patients in the market place.

"See to this soldier first."

"Do not treat him at all," shouts a woman. "He is a thief. Send him away."

Hippocrates looks up from examining a leg wound. "On that blanket," he says quietly. "Wait his turn."

"Treat him at once or I will...."

"Nothing more you can do."

The soldier changes his tune. "Treat him, and I will give you this gold necklace set with emeralds I have here."

"Wait there. The necklace belongs to Alexander's wife. Return it to her," says Hippocrates.

I pause to look at the necklace, and the rich stones glow in the late afternoon sun. I realise instinctively where that necklace came from. Alexander bought it from Timocrates. It must be the one he stole from his mother.

"Gold from the ship," offers the wounded Spartan, writhing in pain.

Hippocrates carries on with his work. A woman takes the necklace, and says, "Are you going to treat a man who has used us so?"

Hippocrates takes fresh bandages. "I treat the sick. It is my art. I do not judge. Am not a god."

Silenus, with a nose for money, sidles up to the soldier, but is rejected.

"Only Hippocrates," groans the Spartan.

That night, the Spartan fleet sails away towards the friendlier port of Cnidus.

But trouble is not finished. Agatha is mightily satisfied to learn of a third problem.

"We must prepare against the plague," says Hippocrates the next day. "The airs will overcome the balance that is within."

"It is too late in the year for the plague," says Nicodemus.

"I have travelled. In Athens I saw the worst plague of our time. Plains people crowded to the city to escape the Spartans. No water. The drains failed. Air was foul.

The plague struck."

"That was summertime."

"Same will happen now. Smell the drains. The fountain is sullied. Its source is stirred with the earth. Boil all water."

As the wounds heal, the people of Astipalea begin to recover a routine out of the chaos.

Yet again, I realise our role in life, a force for good beyond the power of the gods. Stripped of material wealth by the earthquake, the spiritual choice of goodness is clear, like pure spring water, in contrast to the opacity of self-glory.

"Two strained backs recovering well," says Hippocrates.

"So are most of the wounds I have seen," says Nicodemus and moves to the next patient. He looks at the man's face. Then at his chest.

"Open your mouth." He peers down the throat. "Hippocrates, I think you should see this."

One glance at the red eyes, and the seeping spots on the chest is enough.

"Go to your bed. Keep apart from other men."

The patient is the first of many. The plague spreads fast along the blocked sewers and through the smudgy water. It flourishes in the dirt of the rubble, and it flairs in gaudy rashes on the ribs of hungry chests. Where men die in the open, the carrion vultures ignore their bodies.

There is little any doctor can do. We try to keep the sick apart from the healthy, but it is not easy. Preventing the spread is our main concern. Nevertheless, we see every patient, and even though we prescribe nothing, we try to keep the spirit strong.

I have seen thirty-seven people, and return to the remains of Hippocrates' house to get some sleep. Cratis comes towards me, meandering with fatigue.

"You had better get some rest, too, Cratis."

He turns, looking as if he must concentrate to see me. "We are really needed now, Philo. We cannot let patients down."

"You can help no one, Cratis, if you are too tired to walk."

"It is Anaxion. He has the plague. On top of his injuries. He is terrified to die. He asks for me especially. He trusts me, you see."

I watch Cratis walk up the street, a man who is needed.

The fever runs through the town for twenty-nine days. On the thirtieth day, there are five calls fewer.

"Plague turns," says Hippocrates. "Hear Anaxion has rallied."

"Cratis got him through. Gave him the strength."

On the whole, doctors do not get ill as often as other people, something which has long puzzled Hippocrates. But this time, just as we are beginning to feel the problem is coming to an end, one doctor does fall ill.

One piece of the pattern of life, given by Lachesis, the first of the Fates, shifts again. At first, I do not realise what is happening.

It is late in the day when a slave from Cratis's house comes to fetch me. His family has been lucky. Since the house is on the outskirts of the town, it did not suffer as badly in the earthquake as many. It lost only the roof and one wall.

Xenia comes to the gap where the gate was. Her face

is grey and her hair unbraided.

"It is the fever. I sat up all night with him. He burns like a fire and the thirst cannot be quenched."

When I come into the room, Cratis asks Xenia, "Could you make some more barley water?" She goes out to the yard.

I smile at Cratis, noticing the skin of his face is cracked, the eyes red, and his breathing strained. A cotton sheet hides his chest, but I know how that is, too.

"Diagnosis," whispers Cratis. "Tertian fever. Known in severe epidemic form as the plague." He tries to smile. "Prognosis?"

I shake his elbow gently. "Come on."

"Prognosis," says Cratis. "Death."

"Anaxion did not die. You saw to that. And I will see that you do not."

"His was a mild case."

"It was not. Anyway, if you thought you would die, you would not have sent for me."

"I want to speak of another matter," whispers Cratis. He sips some wine from a goblet beside the couch. I have to help him.

"Xenia," he says. "I want you to take care of her. There must be no arranged marriage to make her unhappy again."

"Do not talk like this."

"My eyes are quicker than my tongue, Philo."

"Cratis, there has been nothing between us."

Cratis nods. "She is faithful, I know. But not for the right reason." He turns his head and looks towards the doorway. Outside Xenia is cooking the barley on the outdoor hearth, stirring the pot vehemently.

"I never learned to be at ease with a woman. Xenia's

169

fire, I cannot match it; words are a bridge which, for me, is broken. I am stranded on the far bank. I never talk to any of you either in the way you talk to each other."

"You are talking easily now."

"Yes." Cratis nods. "A candle, which learns to burn only after the sun rises. Ah. Could you write that down somewhere? Xenia did try to help me."

"She was faithful to you, Cratis. It may comfort you to know I would have taken her from you after Lydia died, but she would not come to me."

Cratis smiles, the eyelids so swollen and heavy. "Thank you, Philo, but allow me the dignity of complete truth at the end. It is you that Xenia loves."

"Then you can rest and grow well."

"There is one more thing," says Cratis. "Hanging on the wall there, see that scroll. Odd that it never fell off in the earthquake, a sign perhaps. It is my notes. I have written down all the little truths that Hippocrates comes out with, his little comments like the oracle. I would like him to have them."

"No one else thought of writing them down."

"Men who have not heard Hippocrates can read his words."

We sit together in silence. I have rarely felt so close to another soul; and to Cratis, never.

Hippocrates and I visit him every day, but can find no cure. He is a man who has already made his arrangements.

Cratis dies on the seventh day of his illness.

# CHAPTER FOURTEEN

The moon wanes and grows full again before I return, quite early one morning, to Xenia's house. Beside the road, some heads of corn are ripening, although the crop beyond lies devastated. I look at them, and they are the measure of how I have changed. They are not the gift of Demeter after all, but the certainty of Earth's fertility, the sign that nature cannot be defeated.

Xenia has gathered some pale autumn crocuses and is sitting beside the door, staring down at them.

"I was not sure when to call."

She smiles, but stares still at the crocuses. "I feel so guilty, Philo."

"You have nothing to be guilty about."

"I was too proud. I have not been a good woman. I mocked the gods. They punish me for my hubris. And there is Cratis."

"Yes. I know you must be seen to mourn."

"Not *seen* to mourn. I do mourn, for what Cratis might have been, had the spirit soared. I mourn him, as I would a stillborn child."

"I have come to speak of other things."

"There can be no other things." Xenia looks down at the soft blue flowers in her lap.

And I can find none of the right words.

After the disastrous war with Sparta, Athens loses faith

in her leaders, and the mob rules. The aristocrats move fast and for one hundred and twenty-two days, they rule with a cruel grip, killing those who speak against them, trying to stifle for all time the heady spirit of democracy. But Athens has tasted justice, and will not be whipped into submission. Democratic rule is restored, and wily old warhorse that she is, Athens sets about regaining her power among her allies and among the islands.

So that Sparta might not be tempted to capture the island of Cos and so interrupt the trade route between Athens and Asia, Athenians come to fortify the island, work which must be speedily finished. Athens sends her most able admiral to supervise; she sends Alcibiades.

"Alcibiades is come," is whispered all over the market place. Few, very few indeed, have not *heard* of Alcibiades.

The Admiral of the fleet stands in the market place. "I need food for the men," he says. "And who is a keeper of fine wine on this island?"

"Alexander."

"Then my compliments to Alexander. Tell him that as we are fortifying his island, he may fortify us with his wine." He rides away to supervise the lodging of his men, scattering a group of children playing knucklebones. The hoof of his horse breaks the fingers of a child as he rides on.

"What does Alcibiades think he is doing?" demands Nicodemus, a few days later. "He is building walls round the harbour at Chora at the far end of the island. Chora is little more than a village. He ignores us here in Astipalea."

"Most ships call at Chora these days. It is more than a village, too. The ships like to run up the coast of the mainland. To sail round Cos to Astipalea takes time. Besides we lost so much in the earthquake."

"And another thing," says Nicodemus. "Did you know that Alcibiades deserted the Athenian army, and went over to the Spartans?"

"No-one claims he is good, only that he is extra-ordinary. But why should he do that?" I ask.

"Apparently he insulted the gods when he was drunk, broke up some religious statues. The authorities did not discover who had done it at first, but when they did, they demanded he return from Sicily, and face charges. So he deserted."

And for such a man, Timocrates went to war.

It is late when I reach the house of Alexander. Already he has repaired his home and is living as if the earth-quake had never shaken a stone of the island. Alex-ander has chosen to act as host to the most celebrated, yet most notorious man to come out of the city state of Athens. He has given a lavish dinner party for his own merchant friends, and for Alcibiades. The tables are still laden with plates of figs and apples. The slave boy fills the cups with wine, the flute girls play, and a young man sings tunelessly with a lyre.

I slip in unnoticed among the men in their wreaths of ivy, a tribute to Dionysis, god of wine and song. Alexander lies drunk on his couch, waving his cup in the air to be filled yet again.

Alcibiades, his handsome face only now beginning to harden into new furrows of dissipation and greed, looks arrogantly at his fellow guests and then tries to catch the eye of the youngest flute player. I make my way gradually through the guests and find a place beside him, when his neighbour lurches out of the room.

Alcibiades looks at me with some surprise. I am obviously sober.

"What have we here? Not trouble, I trust."

"No."

"Or perhaps I would welcome trouble. To relieve the boredom of this dull little island." He yawns, and beckons to the flute girl. She pretends not to see him.

"I want to speak with you."

"To see the living legend, eh? And then boast that you know me?"

"No. To find out for myself whether or not Timocrates followed an illusion."

"Timocrates?"

"You will not have heeded him. But he noticed you. You are one reason he chose the path he did."

"I have the power to attract beyond my will," says Alcibiades and sighs, almost as if he wonders what good this has done him.

"Timocrates won the foot race at Olympia the year you came first with the chariot. You will not remember a foot race, won by a man too poor to own even one horse."

Alcibiades sits up lazily, with the sensuous movement of a huge cat. "I do remember Timocrates," he says slowly. "Yes. I was in the stadium when he ran. I remember him very well. I did not know he came from Cos."

I smile. Perhaps that is all Timocrates would have wanted. That Alcibiades had seen him win.

Alcibiades looks round at the drunken men, and then

anew at me beside him. He smiles. "I will tell you something." I realise he confides because he, too, is drunk. "I hated him for it. He is nobody. He is not one of us. He is not bred to lead. And yet he won."

Alcibiades watches the young flute girl leave the party, slipping away, believing herself unnoticed. Alcibiades makes no move; one flute girl is very like another.

Though not, of course, to me. And I close my mind against thoughts of Xenia.

"I will tell you another thing," he says. "He joined the fleet as we sailed for Sicily. I arranged for him to fight under me, not with Nicias."

I say evenly. "But you did not fight at Sicily, did you? You deserted, and joined the Spartan army." I am reckless. To speak to Alcibiades like this is to invite arrest.

"My friend," says Alcibiades lazily. "There was a little matter of my being arrested for insulting the gods. Which is, perhaps, why I forgive your words now. Yes, I deserted, but Athens could not wait to take me back. They have no other general like me."

"Timocrates is dead."

Alcibiades stretches, and holds out his cup for more wine.

"Really? And I live." He frowns, as if trying to recall an elusive memory, some small irritation in his mind, something which seems contradictory. He gives up and laughs. "Of course, there *is* a difference between us."

The fortification of Chora goes well. New houses are built as the Athenians stack up the protective harbour walls. Our own house is rebuilt, but it is not like it used to be. Every man who has ever cut a stone or laid a brick becomes a master builder. Those who have not are apprentices. The women run the farms and, for a while, the pattern of life is turned upside down. We spend time in Chora. Our trade is in strained muscles in the back and shoulder. Men are too busy to fall ill with disease.

Not everyone is happy with the arrangements. Unable to come to terms with the devastation of our town, some men join those who founded a new life on the island to the west of our shores, which they call Astipalea.

Agatha comes one day from the market. "Know who is going to the island now?" she demands, bursting with gossip. "Cratis's family. His father is a broken man, you know. Terrible tragedy to lose your only son."

"Who, exactly, is going?" I ask casually.

"Well, all of them. The father's brothers. Their wives. And Xenia, too. I suppose she is useful to them. Though they say she is quite changed. She will see no-one."

I call at the house and ask to speak to Xenia. The message comes back that she will not come out of her room. "Xenia is rather quiet these days," a relative tries to explain. "She lives in the hands of fate."

Under the plane tree, Hippocrates stares out across the market place. "The traders drift to Chora," he observes. "Eastern aspect. Very healthy."

"Why are you smiling, Hippocrates? Our patients begin to desert us."

"Tomorrow," he says, "we go to the Asclepium."

We arrive at the temple of healing before midday and are greeted by Hicetas dressed in a white, woollen cloak. Theodorus has returned to the mainland. Hicetas, now the chief priest, looks tired and old.

Over a simple meal of dried fish and bread, eaten in the cool of the portico, Hippocrates introduces the subject on his mind.

"Not many priests about."

"Or patients," adds Nicodemus.

I glance up to the temple on the terrace above, and see that the door stands open, very slightly. Silently, it closes. Someone has been watching us.

With the pillars of the portico casting stripes of shade upon his face, Hicetas says, "We take our powers from the first Asclepium at Epidaurus. The snakes, in the beginning, came from there. It is many years now that we have practised our art on this island. Sometimes we have many patients, other times a few."

"But never so few as today?" Nicodemus presses the point.

Hicetas inclines his head. "We have lost some of our following, but only those who are beyond our spiritual power. Some found help from the Great Doctor. This we accept."

"The future lies with us," says Nicodemus, and some of the old disdain shows on his face.

Hicetas frowns. "It is the god, Asclepius, who heals. And he works through his chosen."

"We are each chosen," says Hippocrates gently.

"As you probably know, we plan to move to Chora," says Nicodemus. "Our students must be where the patients are. Perhaps we can work together more closely."

"You want the healing snakes," says the young priest.

"Snakes are the last thing I want," says Nicodemus.

"How many priests have you now?" I ask.

There is a pause. "Three," admits Hicetas, "and Aspasia."

The young priest speaks again. "I believe Aspasia lacks the power which comes from Asclepius himself. It is her fault we have fallen so low."

Hicetas says, "I have told you before, I will have none of this talk. If we do not trust Aspasia, who interprets the dreams, where will we be?" He turns to Hippocrates. "You must understand we are committed to our form of healing, a healing of long tradition."

"Three priests," says Hippocrates slowly. "Need more if we join you."

"More?" says Hicetas.

"Of course."

"Not less?"

"Perhaps ten more."

"Hmm. More priests."

"You have those with the gift for tending the earth," says Nicodemus. "We need herbs. We need food. There is room for gardens. That will be nothing compared to the spiritual counselling. We have not forgotten how you cured Medea by giving her spiritual peace."

At last Hicetas smiles. "More priests," he says. "It will be the rebirth of our order." He looks to the younger priest. "We might agree," he says.

"It is settled then?" asks Nicodemus.

"There may be a problem," says Hicetas cautiously. "Aspasia."

"We will talk with her," says Hippocrates.

"I believe she may refuse. Perhaps if you go to the temple and prostrate yourselves, it may placate her."

"I will make an offering to Asclepius," says Hippocrates, "but you understand I cannot revere Aspasia."

With gifts of grain and oil for the god, we climb to the temple. The door stands open, waiting for us. In the inner room, offerings lie on the table in front of the screen from behind which Aspasia might appear. But we are left looking at each other.

"I am not lying on my face for that fraud," mutters Nicodemus.

Hippocrates says, "The priests and doctors will unite for the greater benefit of the Asclepium."

For an answer, a snake slides across the marble floor and makes for Nicodemus.

"Get away from me," he says loudly.

I pick up the snake and carry it outside.

But Aspasia does not lower herself to speak in person, she sends a message through the youngest priest. The request is impossible to meet, since she alone has power; she alone controls the snakes.

"We can ignore her," says Nicodemus. "Just move in."

"No," say the priests, even the one who earlier spoke against Aspasia.

Hicetas says, "In her is invested much power, even if she does not fully have the gift to heal. She will call upon Poseidon to destroy the Asclepium, as she called on him to save it during the earthquake."

"She has no more power than you," says Hippocrates.

"She keeps the snakes," says the young priest, as if that explains everything.

"Try again tomorrow," Hippocrates says with scant conviction.

The couches are covered with brightly coloured woven quilts, and the floor is strewn with sweet herbs. In each room burns a lamp with plenty of oil. I am wondering if the dream will ever be ours when I hear a noise.

Nicodemus stands outside the door, swathed in a black cloak. He hands me a second wrap.

"Come with me. We will arrange the future."

The air is warm and absolutely still. I love the feel of the night here. "It is too warm for a cloak."

"Put it on, all the same." He carries a stick and a small bowl. "Poppy. I took it from the pharmacy. I have spoken with the young priest to discover the snakes are kept in a pit very near the temple. Now, how much poppy would put a snake to sleep for half the night?"

"What for?"

"The young priest does not guard his tongue."

"So?"

"Each night, at midnight, Aspasia goes alone to the temple. She pours libations, and asks the god to keep her powerful. While she is at the table, we shall be in the back room, learning a trick from Timocrates."

I begin to understand.

The dark cloaks disguise us as we creep up to the higher terrace to locate the pit where the snakes coil and writhe, when they are not busy healing.

"We cannot be scientific. We have made no observations. Hippocrates would not approve," says Nicodemus.

His method is to dip the end of the stick into the powdered poppy, then push it down to the snakes, teasing out the flickering tongues to lick the drug. There is little light left but we can just about see what we are doing.

We wait and all but one snake stops writhing about. Nicodemus can scarcely see but he prods again with his poppy-anointed pole and we glimpse the slash of a forked tongue. At last they all sleep.

We creep to the temple and wait in the inner room until midnight.

Eventually the door opens and Aspasia slips inside. She pours her libation onto the floor, and raises her hands to the roof. We can see her only by the light coming through the open door.

"Mighty Asclepius, I have served you well these years. Renew in me your great power of healing."

Nicodemus leans forward to the speaking vents, and says, "No more, Aspasia." His voice has a wonderful echo to it.

Aspasia takes a long-handled hook from the corner.

Eventually, she whispers, "But I have the snakes."

Nicodemus leans forward again. "The snakes, Aspasia. I have taken the snakes."

Aspasia takes a long-handled hook from the corner and leaves the temple. We watch her from within its shadow. She walks across to the pit, and with the hook, hauls out a snake. It dangles still and lifeless.

"Eeeeeeeee." The scream is chilling and sinister as from an injured animal in the night.

We hear running feet, the soft feet of a small light body.

Down the steps she goes, hair flying, her scarlet priestess robe clutched up so that she can run faster. She races across the terrace, young and unholy as she is, and down to the gate which is never locked. She disappears through it, into the night of the forest, the enchanted forest where no-one might die, and none are born. Nothing follows her, and she does not return.

*       *       *

The next morning there is amazement among the priests.

"Aspasia has gone," says Hicetas. "Fled the temple. The door stands open."

"The snakes," asks Nicodemus innocently, "has she taken them with her?"

"No. No, they remain. They are rather apathetic, as if they know their mentor has fled."

The young priest speaks. "Aspasia has relinquished her powers. She will never return. It is a sign we shall be great again."

Hicetas says, smiling, "Asclepius has arranged a miracle cure for *us*. Hippocrates and I will take our morning meal together. Prepare bread and fish and fowl, some cheese, and perhaps honey cake, as well, to suit the occasion."

Nicodemus catches my eye. "Thank you, great Asclepius," he says.

On the way home, we pause in Chora market place in a shady place under a plane tree. "We may have our medical school, but I will still lecture to the public. And this seems a likely spot." Hippocrates sits down.

I watch the pattern of leaves dodging across his face and he looks no different from the first time I saw him, sitting under another plane tree in the old town.

A leaf falls on his knee. "See? A gift. Yes, this is my tree."

Mother takes my hands. "I hear Xenia leaves this afternoon."

I run all the way to the harbour. I see, from a distance, the family are aboard. The boatman is impatient to catch the tide. Only Xenia stands on the shore.

"Xenia," I shout, and run towards her.

She stares beyond the boat, towards the western horizon. Her eyes see another place, in a different time.

I arrive and still she waits, with the boatmen bellowing at her.

"Xenia. You cannot go." I stop. Her eyes do not take me in.

Slowly, she says, "The sea. Look at its power. We are nothing against the tide. We are lost to fate."

"You are stronger than fate. You freed *yourself* from slavery, Xenia."

"I did. Yes, I did."

"I am your home, Xenia."

The mists of confusion in her eyes seem to clear a little.

"A boat can be steered through the water. Timocrates and I went to Olympia."

"And Nicodemus cured Menon," she remembers.

She turns to me, and I watch her face come alive once more.

"How bright the windows, Xenia. How clearly we see each other in them. I understand what you said about love, now."

The other land and alien time drop away, and she smiles as if waking up. "I was right all the time."

We laugh like children.

"I got to the boat," she whispers. "I almost went. But I am found."

"You want to stay with Philo, then?" shouts Cratis's father from the boat, impatient to be away. He sees Xenia as a burden.

The boatman turns and bellows, "You are Philo, are you? I have a message from one, Timocrates, in Athens. 'Make certain Alexander does not sell the necklace.'"

So I had been right when I had seen that gold and emerald necklace that the Spartan had stolen. Alexander had bought both my father's couch, and Timocrates' mother's necklace.

As Xenia and I walk back to my house, we are almost too happy to think about anyone else. But Xenia says, "Why would Timocrates remember the necklace in Athens when he was about to go to war?"

"I cannot imagine. It sounds as if he wanted to get it back. He must have had a bad conscience. It is sad, you know, that Timocrates should have died with that on his mind."

"Could it be...?"

"What?"

"Could it be he went to Athens *after* the war?"

"Do not create false hopes, Xenia. Remember, a man actually saw the javelin strike him dead."

"Yes, I know. I suppose I have never been able to believe it."

That the message does not make sense is forgotten.

Soon after the wedding, we will move, with Leon, Mother and Agatha, to a house that is being built in Chora.

Meanwhile, there is much work in our medical school at the Asclepium.

I do not understand how she comes to be there, but one morning I find Agatha holding forth to Hicetas.

"I have never been wrong with geese," she says. "And I knew the plague would come. Earthquake, Spartans; so there had to be a third."

"Are you trained?" asks Hicetas, puzzled.

"Certainly not. It is in here." Agatha taps her head.

"Do you, by any chance, have a response to snakes?"

"Yes. They should be exterminated."
Hicetas looks disappointed.

Delphia, too, drifts to Chora. She corners Hippocrates
by the gate to the Asclepium. "All these years old
Delphi give you power to magic, and you cast me off.
Spit me out, like a chewy onion."

"No, Delphia. I would never cast you off. But the
herbs grow here now."

"Like a broken shoe." Delphia looks like an ill-girded
parcel, falling apart. Power through the plants held
her together.

Hippocrates takes a deep breath. "Will you be my
adviser? About herbs."

Delphia cackles. "No good without me, eh Hippocrati?"

"In secret, of course. The priests will be...jealous of
you."

She hobbles off. Nicodemus says, "There goes the
only person who ever got the better of Hippocrates."

The Asclepium provides the perfection after which all
men should strive; excellence of the mind, the spirit,
and the body.

Here lies knowledge, the opportunity for contempla-
tion with the inner soul, and the means to a healthy
life. Now at last we have a room for operations;
another for setting bones, with Nicodemus' great
wooden frame standing in the middle.

We even have a library in which we can work.
Hippocrates and I hang the scrolls on its walls, remembering how we came by each. We have well over
forty.

"These scrolls will inform doctors for all time; yet to

me, they are my past. Who else but Cratis would have
written down your aphorisms? Your little sayings? And
Nicodemus' paper on treating club foot. He learned
more than how to bandage."

"Look at this." Hippocrates hands me Timocrates'
writing on training for a healthy body. 'Exercise and
diet.' Dear Timocrates.

My rival at Olympia, my friend in everything else.

It is weird to know that for eternity, men will take of
the medical knowledge stored here, but will know nothing about us. Or how the papers came about.

As Nicodemus and I return from the barber where we
are spruced up for my wedding this evening, we notice
a cargo caique unloading. Few ships come in here, to
Astipalea, these days. A passenger limps off.

For a moment, Nicodemus pauses. He shakes his
head, and we move on.

I ask no dowry, for Xenia is the property of no-one.

"My wedding gift." I give her the knuckle bones I
always carry with me in the medical bag she sewed
herself.

"A bond that has always been," she says. She moves
serenely across the yard, but her eyes are not quiet,
they dance with joy. She hugs Agatha. "You will have
to do as I say now, Agatha."

"You, mistress of the home," she sniffs. "Well, it is
not unfitting. Not unfitting at all."

We make a sacrifice to Hestia on the hearth.

"We really should call on Demeter at the same
time," says Mother.

"This is the work of Hestia, Mother," and I look at
Leon holding Xenia's hand, and remember my

supplication.

"Very well." But I see her spill a little wine deliberately, a libation to her proven friend. Xenia nods.

The smoke dances up into the evening sky, and I am confused. We have done much, Xenia and I, to mould our own lives. But something else has created this beautiful pattern. And I cannot believe it is the whim of a god. There is goodness here. Might there be some greater power than they?

But my flow of ideas is broken. Hippocrates is about to empty a bowl of grain over us, when the gate of the house is flung open.

Timocrates limps into the yard. "I return to you," he says. "I have come home."

I let go of Xenia's hand, and can only stare at him. There is a complete silence of disbelief which no-one seems able to break. Timocrates, gaunt and older, stares round at each of us in turn, but with the joy on his face I saw before only when he won the crown of wild olive.

Xenia is the first to recover and runs to hug him. Then we are all laughing together, and slapping him on the back, and asking questions all at the same time.

"Always did have a nose for food," says Agatha.

Xenia takes him by the hand and hauls him over to a couch. She brings him a plate of chicken and vegetables. "Eat up and explain everything."

"You are supposed to be dead," Agatha tells him severely.

"I did nearly die. But a javelin recognises its master. A Sicilian girl took me in and, when I felt better, I caught up with the retreating army, helping the sick who escaped. There were not many."

"And you went to Athens *after* the war?" I remember

the message from the boatman, and now it makes sense. "You found your father?"

"Yes."

"Did he acknowledge you?" asks Nicodemus.

"He did."

"And?"

"We did not like each other very much," Timocrates shrugs. "Could any man live up to the image I created? And I lack Athenian graces. But I stayed long enough to collect money off him to buy back my mother's necklace. He paid to get rid of me, I think."

"Have a pear," says Xenia, pressing food upon him, wanting to restore him to his former glowing beauty.

"Will you stay?" asks Hippocrates.

"Yes." There is no hesitation.

"What changed your mind?"

"Helping the wounded on that filthy journey back. I saved life, when others could not. Yes, I stay to work alongside you."

"Thank you." Hippocrates' voice is gruff and my throat feels blocked by apples.

"Men do not show tears," sniffs Agatha, and the sniff sounds very moist.

Hippocrates puts an arm round each of our shoulders and beckons Nicodemus over. "Children of Apollo. I am so proud."

And I stretch out my hands to Xenia and Mother, for whatever the sorrows we have each experienced, we stand together now, enveloped in the golden light of the god. We must drink the essence of the moment to the full.

# POSTSCRIPT

All fiction must search after truth, but facts can be more reassuring.

Hippocrates, known as the father of medicine, was a real person, living in the fifth century BC, often in Cos, but also travelling elsewhere in Greece. He did have students, who formed a medical school, possibly on the lines of this story, though no other medical character in the novel is factual.

Our knowledge of him is based on about sixty papers, known as the *Hippocratic corpus*, which exist from this period, none of them proven to be written by Hippocrates, but several attributed to him, or to those who followed his methods. The papers are a mixture of case notes, lectures, medical diaries and theoretical treatises on a variety of subjects and form the basis of the medical details of this book.

It is true that before the influence of Hippocrates, medicine was a branch of philosophy. Hippocrates developed his ideas as a separate art, based on close observation of the patient, study of case notes, prognosis, and the belief that no medicine was better than wrong medicine. He believed that the body is capable of helping itself to heal, and medicine must assist this natural progress, which is precisely the way the recently developed drug, interferon, works.

Hippocrates had many fascinating modern insights into medicine, over four hundred years before the birth of Christ. His recorded crisis days in pneumonia were observed until the discovery of modern drugs. He had a regime for health, based on diet and exercise. He advised against eating too many eggs. He noted that milk can cause headaches. Only recently have dairy products been accused of causing migraine.

Although he had no knowledge of a virus or bacteria, he did observe that something in the air caused epidemics, and that brackish water led to dysentery. The whole of one paper, 'Airs, waters, places', reads like a public health report.

While a great deal of medicine was directed towards reducing fever, Hippocrates observed that the heat was necessary for the body to overcome infection. He prescribed willow and ash bark, and these contain salicylic acid which today is an ingredient of aspirin.

Perhaps, even more important, medical ethics are enshrined in the Hippocratic oath, an oath universally sworn until this century.